the murder code

(a remi laurent fbi suspense thriller—book 2)

ava strong

Ava Strong

Debut author Ava Strong is author of the REMI LAURENT mystery series, comprising three books (and counting); of the ILSE BECK mystery series, comprising four books (and counting); and of the STELLA FALL psychological suspense thriller series, comprising three books (and counting).

An avid reader and lifelong fan of the mystery and thriller genres, Ava loves to hear from you, so please feel free to visit www.avastrongauthor.com to learn more and stay in touch.

ISBN: 978-1-0943-9295-0

BOOKS BY AVA STRONG

REMI LAURENT FBI SUSPENSE THRILLER
THE DEATH CODE (Book #1)
THE MURDER CODE (Book #2)
THE MALICE CODE (Book #3)

ILSE BECK FBI SUSPENSE THRILLER
NOT LIKE US (Book #1)
NOT LIKE HE SEEMED (Book #2)
NOT LIKE YESTERDAY (Book #3)
NOT LIKE THIS (Book #4)

STELLA FALL PSYCHOLOGICAL SUSPENSE THRILLER
HIS OTHER WIFE (Book #1)
HIS OTHER LIE (Book #2)
HIS OTHER SECRET (Book #3)

PROLOGUE

East Hampton, Long Island
2:15 a.m.

What a victory.

The painting was everything he had hoped for and more.

It was all so clear, all so obvious to anyone who knew what to look for.

Of course, only the select few knew *how* to look.

Billionaire Montgomery Dyson stood alone in the East Gallery of one of his mansions, staring at his latest acquisition. A warm summer breeze wafted through the screen window, bringing with it the sharp smell of salt water and the shush of Atlantic surf. On the walls hung paintings from the greatest eras of Western Civilization—a delicate little portrait of the Virgin and Child from 14th century Florence, its tempera paint still retaining its brilliant colors through the centuries, a 15th century engraving by Albrecht Dürer, and later works by Rembrandt and Matisse and Van Gogh. On a gilded table that once graced the interior of Versailles stood a bronze statue by Rodin.

Dyson noticed none of these things. He had eyes only for his latest acquisition. An art collector for most of his sixty-eight years, he would have given up all of his vast collection to own the painting he gazed at now.

It showed the figure of Death riding a red horse through a starry sky. The figure seemed huge, taking up most of the painting and dominating the little village below. A few lights shone in the cottages. A farmer, late returning from his fields, drove his ox cart along a dirt lane, unaware of the terror that rode above. At the lower right corner of the frame stood a country manor with stone turrets and a spacious garden. Bright lights shone from a series of picture windows in one wing, hinting that a party was in progress.

Death appeared to be heading for the manor. He had one arm raised high, the cruel curve of his scythe framing a constellation in the night sky.

"Fascinating," Dyson murmured, studying the stars in the painting.

He went over to a mahogany bookshelf and retrieved a leather-bound volume. Flipping through the pages, he glanced at the painting and then back at the book.

"No, no," he muttered to himself, flipping further on in the book.

His eyes lit up.

"Ah! Could it be?" he looked at the illustration on the page, then at the painting, and back at the page. "Yes! I do believe it is."

The sound of the door opening behind him, but nothing more, as if someone was hesitating before coming further.

"I don't need anything, Winston, thank you," Dyson said without turning around.

The door closed. He heard a soft tread across the 18th century Persian rug.

Irritated, Dyson turned.

"I said, I—"

The words froze in his throat.

A stranger stood in the middle of the room. He wore a monk's robe with the cowl obscuring his face.

Dyson did not notice much more, for his gaze was drawn to the scythe the man carried, an antique that looked like it had once reaped wheat at some nineteenth-century farmstead.

"What do you want?" Dyson croaked. He felt the urge to scream for help, but the sight of that rust-dappled blade, its edge newly sharpened, made him keep his voice down.

The cowled man pointed to the painting, then the book that had dropped at Dyson's feet. The hand looked powerful, with thick fingers, yet well-manicured.

When Dyson didn't move, the intruder took another step forward, his monk's robe making a soft rustle. The hand that had pointed now grasped the scythe.

Dyson raised his hands, both as a sign of surrender and to ward off any blow and took a step to the left.

The man gestured with the scythe, as if to indicate that Dyson should move more.

"Wait!" Dyson said, temporarily overcoming his fear. "Don't take the painting. Anything but that. Take the book if you want. Take anything else."

The intruder gestured again.

"You want money? I can give you millions. Just don't—"

The man in the monk's robes raised his scythe.

Dyson trembled, then firmed up his resolve. A lifetime of study and searching. He wasn't going to give that up. No. Never.

He moved to get between the stranger and his treasured painting.

"I'll give you anything," Dyson said. "But you can't—"

The stranger turned the scythe and hit Dyson on the shoulder with the back end. The billionaire staggered to the side.

The sudden pain killed his resolve. He was a man of great resources, and he could hire private detectives to hunt down this madman and get back what was his.

The intruder must have realized the same thing because he took two long strides forward and brought the scythe down on him.

Dyson raised his arms to shield his head from the blow.

The first cut nearly severed his right forearm. Dyson gasped and fell to his knees, clutching his arm.

He didn't even see the stroke that cut deep into his neck, severing his carotid artery and spraying blood all over a sketch by Caillebotte.

Dyson sank to the floor. The intruder raised his scythe a third time, then stopped.

There was no need. Montgomery Dyson was dead.

CHAPTER ONE

Professor Remi Laurent shuffled her lecture notes and prepared to finish her class on medieval religious symbolism. The usual collection of bored undergraduates sat arrayed before her. Unfortunately, this class could be used to fulfill the undergraduate art history requirement, so it attracted more than the usual quota of utterly uninterested freshmen.

At least she enjoyed the anticipation of some great Italian cuisine and her boyfriend's expert lovemaking later in the evening. For a middle-aged man, Professor Cyril Mullen was remarkably virile and uninhibited. Being with him made her feel like she was in her twenties again, except for the constant badgering about setting a wedding date. She got more torn about that with every day.

Do your job and worry about that later, she told herself.

"All right, let's look at the next slide," she said, trying to ignore the several students who held their phones beneath their desks and were busy texting.

Remi turned on the last slide of her PowerPoint presentation.

"Let's talk a bit about the symbolism of color in Renaissance painting. We'll be getting more into this next time, but I wanted to give you a taste today. Meaning was not only determined by the symbolism of color itself, but practical matters such as the cost of the pigments. Take blue, for example. Here we have the Martinengo Altarpiece painted by Lorenzo Lotto around the year 1516. The Virgin Mary holds the baby Jesus and is flanked by various figures, including an adult Jesus with stigmata.

"Note the greatest use of blue is on the Virgin Mary's dress. The only other figures wearing blue are the adult Jesus and the two angels flying above. Blue was reserved for the holiest figures at this time because blue was the most expensive paint. It was made from lapis lazuli, which had to be imported all the way from Afghanistan."

A hand shot up. Remi recognized an archaeology student, an intelligent young woman who actually did the assigned reading.

"Isn't lapis lazuli what the ancient Egyptians used to decorate the mask of Tutankhamun?"

It wasn't really a question. More of a statement. The student was always overly eager to show off her knowledge.

Remi forgave her. At least the young woman *had* some knowledge.

"Yes, it was. Lapis lazuli was used extensively in ancient Egypt. I can't speak to the symbolism of it in that culture, though. A bit before my time."

She laughed at her little joke. None of her students did.

One young man near the back of her class raised his hand.

"Yes?"

"Did you read about that killer who was after the cryptex?"

Remi tensed. That crazed man had murdered several people in his quest for the medieval device and came within moments of unlocking its secrets.

She had helped bring him to justice, and that action had given her more pride and sense of accomplishment than any of her academic laurels.

Luckily, it hadn't brought her any media attention. Yet.

"Yes, of course I heard about it," she replied, nervously brushing back her hair.

"Did they, like, call you or anything?"

"No, why would they?"

"Well, like, you've talked about the cryptex a lot. You're a total expert, right?"

"I don't know much about the case. Only what I read in the news. I suspect the FBI caught him through their usual methods."

Such a bringing in an expert civilian advisor, she thought with pride.

"So you didn't get involved in the case?" the student pressed.

"No." Remi turned to the screen again. "Now the important thing to remember about the Renaissance is that symbolism was sometimes constrained by cost, and that artists had to work within certain practical parameters while still needing to express as much meaning as they could. We'll see that artists of the period became adept at introducing many layers of meaning into their works. That's all for today—" a rumbling of closed books and shifting chairs drowned out her next words, so she turned up the microphone.

Feedback screeched through the speakers. Her students winced.

Remi smiled. Not as effective as a new piece of chalk on a blackboard, but good enough.

"Please read chapter five for next time."

The students paused. When they saw that she wasn't going to say any more, they rushed for the door, many already pulling out their phones.

Remi sighed and packed away her papers. Every lecture here made her miss the Sorbonne even more. The students there were the best of the best, already well read and eager to learn more.

But she shouldn't complain, Remi thought as she followed the last of her students out of the lecture hall. Georgetown paid well, gave her travel grants for her research, and she got to be with Cyril.

It also indirectly led to her involvement in an FBI case, something she never would have dreamed she'd ever get involved with. That's what the student had been referring to.

She scanned the crowd for that student, hoping he wouldn't stop her in the hall and ask her more questions. Remi had never been very good at lying.

To her relief, she spotted the back of his head a good fifty meters away. He was hurrying out of the building as quickly as the rest of them.

Tension eased from her, replaced by anticipation as she hurried upstairs to her office. Done with her last class of the day, she could get back to her real vocation—figuring out the secret of the cryptex.

What that student didn't know, what no one knew, was that as FBI agent Daniel Walker and the police led the killer away, she had taken her few precious moments alone with the device to unlock it, using the code the killer himself had discovered.

She almost ran down the hallway to her office, absentmindedly returning a greeting from one of her passing colleagues before nearly bumping into another, then closed herself inside and locked the door. She wanted no interruptions.

Remi turned on her computer, opened up a file misnamed "Family Photos" in order to fool any prying eyes, and scrolled down through subfolders labeled "Summer 2019" and "Farm Trips" to a folder labeled "Bridgette's Eighth Birthday."

She had no eight-year-old relative named Bridgette.

Opening it up, she came to the six photos she had taken on that night.

The first two were blurry, with the cryptex partially out of frame. She had been so nervous after finally opening it, she could barely control her phone.

The next four were clear and in focus. She opened one up.

Engraved on the ivory interior of the cryptex was a map. A little town stood next to a meandering river. A row of hills or mountains stood a bit to the right, angling across the map and giving the indication that the range continued off both ends.

Across the river from the town and a little downstream or upstream, was a spot marked with an X.

In the lower righthand corner was the floorplan of a church. Halfway down the nave was another X.

She leaned back and smiled. For several days she had spent all her waking hours—and many of the hours when she should have been sleeping—trying to figure out the location of this town and church. There was no label, no writing on the inside of the cryptex at all. Whoever opened the device was supposed to know what town and church it showed.

Remi, of course, did not. So she had spent countless hours searching on Google Earth as well as several old maps of medieval and Renaissance Europe to find a match.

It had been no simple task. Over the seven centuries since the map had been etched inside the cryptex, rivers had changed course, towns had come and gone, and churches had disappeared or been remodeled beyond recognition.

Remi had kept at it, studying, crosschecking, looking up the floor plan of every church she could that dated to the correct century.

Perseverance had won out at last.

She had found the church. It still stood in the Tuscan countryside not far from Florence. The river was still there with a slightly altered course thanks to a dam built by Mussolini in the late twenties, and the town still survived as well.

The Church of Saint Pantaleon of Nicomedia had been built in the early 13th century, dedicated to the patron saint of physicians. A convert from paganism in late 3rd century, when the Roman Empire was still persecuting Christians, he worked as a physician in the court of the Emperor Galerius Maximianus. He lost that job soon enough after he professed his faith and started worked miracles of healing. He was eventually martyred along with several other local Christians in the year 303.

What struck her most about this story was where he as from. Nicomedia was a city within the Roman Empire in what is now northwestern Turkey. All but vanished today, it had once briefly been the capital of the Eastern Roman Empire and a hotbed of early Christian activity.

Including the activity of another saint, Saint Adrian.

On their last case, they had caught a clergyman from the Monastery of St. Adrian of Nicomedia near Ravenna, northern Italy. Remi had discovered that this order of monks was dedicated to protecting the secret of the cryptex. Indeed, they had caught the man trying to steal it, which would have certainly been a sin if he hadn't been trying to keep it out of the hands of a serial killer.

Now the cryptex was in the hands of the Vatican. She wondered whatever happened to that clergyman, who had been let go, and his ancient religious order.

She also wondered about the connection of Nicomedia. St. Adrian was martyred only three years after Saint Pantaleon, and in the same city. Had they known each other?

Remi pulled up the church's saved location on Google Maps and studied it for the hundredth time. Yes, it must be the right place. The cryptex map was far from precise, but there was the same angle of the river and hills, the same relative location of town and church. It had to be the right one.

The only thing that made her doubt was that she did not have an accurate 14th century map of the church. The only published map she could track down was from a book from the early 20th century. Its reconstruction of the various phases of the church were all speculative. Excavations in 2007 had probably revealed much more information, but that excavation report had never been published, an irritating habit among archaeologists. To read the manuscript she'd have to go to the archives in Florence.

Remi planned to do just that. Once she figured out how to ask for and receive a week off, she'd go to Italy and track down the manuscript. She had taken a lot of time off for the FBI case, and she wasn't really in a position to ask for more leave.

She'd have to find a way, though. This was her life's work. After she had read up on as many details of the church and its construction as possible and earned freedom from teaching for a week, she'd go there and see what that X marked.

Assuming it marked anything. Like so many churches, it had been expanded and restored several times over the centuries, and then modern archaeologists had come with their test pits and subsurface imaging. There was a good chance that whatever the cryptex had marked got dug up years ago, perhaps centuries ago.

No, don't think like that. You've come too far, risked too much, to be put off now.

She pulled up some articles on early Renaissance Tuscany and started to read, giving herself more background into the ecclesiastic politics of the region at the time the cryptex had been made. As a researcher she knew that a broad base of knowledge could always help in unexpected ways. Since she had nothing more to read about the Church of Saint Pantaleon of Nicomedia itself, delving into the context in which it was built might provide some insight.

Excitement drove her on. Ever since that FBI case, she had found academic life, once so cozy and intellectually stimulating, a bit dull. Following the trail of the cryptex added some spice to her otherwise predictable days.

She kept reading.

The alarm on her phone buzzed. A quarter to seven already? She had promised to meet Cyril at seven. She had been so preoccupied with her studies recently that she had been late for several dates. That irritated her lover and a couple of times he had come to her office to find her.

She couldn't have that. She didn't want Cyril to see what she was doing.

Turning off her computer and locking up her office, she felt a sting of guilt for deceiving him. He was a good man, always kind and attentive to her, and a great father to the daughter he had with his first wife.

Their divorce had not been a clean one. Cyril rarely talked about it. Remi had never met Trisha, the ex-wife, and never wanted to.

Whatever the source of the breakup, at least Cyril had stayed devoted to his teenaged girl. Thursday evenings and every other weekend were what he called "sacred times" with her. Remi never saw him then.

Yes, a good man, and those were hard to find. You should appreciate them, and certainly never lie to them.

And yet, she thought as she walked downstairs past a janitor mopping the floor, something held her back from telling him the whole truth. While he didn't mock her research into the cryptex, he didn't exactly respect it either. He always tried to steer her toward "more serious fields of interest."

Besides, she kind of liked having a secret. Not even Daniel Walker, the FBI agent she had worked with on the Cryptex Killer case, knew she had opened the cryptex and photographed it.

Just as well that she did open it, because the Vatican had bought the device from the museum where it had been discovered hidden inside another object. She didn't know how many millions they gave the museum, but she would bet all those millions that no researcher outside the Holy See would ever get to handle the cryptex again.

Cyril waited for her outside the building, holding his briefcase. Unlike most academics, he didn't carry a satchel or backpack, but a businessman's briefcase. There had always been something businesslike about Cyril.

"Did you score any meth?" Remi asked, using one of the only American slang terms she knew.

"Excellent batch," Cyril said. "One of my incisors fell out just five minutes ago."

It was the old joke. Two nights a week Cyril, one of the most respected historians of his generation, volunteered at an adult literacy program, teaching rehab single mothers their ABCs. Despite her little joke, this work put Cyril on a pedestal in her eyes.

It also put her own problems in perspective. If these uneducated women could stop taking one of the street's most addictive products, Remi should be able to solve a medieval puzzle.

Their fingers interlaced for moment before releasing. Then they walked down the path by the side of the quad together, close but not too close. In American universities, one had to be careful to keep up appearances.

Because of this, they kept their conversation professional, talking about the agenda of an upcoming faculty meeting and what they were researching at the moment. Remi found herself feeling guilty.

You love this man and you're even planning on marrying him, she told herself. *You need to tell him about your discovery. He'll be excited. Happy for you.*

Remi was not convinced about this last part. In fact, when she had told him she wasn't researching the cryptex anymore, he had approved. Like everyone else, he thought her talents could be better spent elsewhere.

Remi worried about his reaction if she told him. No, *when* she told him.

She needed his approval for the travel funds to Florence, after all.

He wouldn't say no, would he?

That's uncharitable. He cares about you.

"You've grown quiet," Cyril said.

Remi managed a smile. "We'll have plenty of time to talk over dinner."

"Yes we will," Cyril said, his hand brushing hers. "We have some important matters to discuss."

Remi's heart beat a little faster, a mix of emotions going through her. He wanted to set a date, and she needed to bring up a sore point about her research.

But she had to. She had to get to the bottom of this.

"Butterflies?" Cyril asked with a smile.

"What do you mean butterflies?"

Cyril laughed. "American expression. Butterflies in the stomach. It means you're nervous."

"Yes. Butterflies in the stomach."

But not for the reason you think.

CHAPTER TWO

FBI Agent Daniel Walker of the Antiquities Division surveyed the murder scene. He had never been in the Hamptons before, and the bloody body of a billionaire was not the best introduction to one of America's most expensive zip codes.

The murder had happened more than eight hours ago. CSI had already done their thing and taken away the body. Since the FBI had become involved, the body should have stayed in place so he could get a firsthand view of it, but Montgomery Dyson was no ordinary murder victim. The file said he was the twenty-seventh richest man in the United States, a billionaire owning a vast real estate empire inherited from his father. He had seven homes, three yachts, a private jet, a Swiss bank account, and God knows what else.

Odd that Daniel had never heard of him. The company did not bear his name and a quick Google turned up almost nothing. No flashy donations, no directorships other than for his own company, not even anything in the society pages. Every other rich guy with a tenth of his net worth was all over the Internet.

Which made Daniel wonder what Mr. Dyson had been up to.

Collecting art, for one. "The East Gallery," as the house staff called it to distinguish it from "The West Gallery" (because why have just one?) looked like a small-scale city museum. Italian Renaissance, Dutch masters, French Impressionists. The guy had taste.

Which brought Daniel to a significant gap on the wall that showed nothing but a hook and enough room to fit a medium-sized painting.

That was the only thing missing.

Wait. Maybe not. A shelf of antiquarian books, none of them looking like they were less than a couple of hundred years old, sat beneath a landscape by Manet. The books were tightly shelved, advisable so the pages wouldn't get warped by moisture, except for one gap. A book of about two inches thickness was missing. A hefty tome, or two less hefty tomes.

Daniel took a turn about the room. There were no books anywhere else but the shelf. Dyson, or more likely his servants, kept the room neat and tidy. A gap in the bookshelf most likely meant a missing book.

The CSI team had already given him a rundown of the rest of the house—no signs of forced entry, no other people killed, and a trail of bloodstains leading from the East Gallery to the pool.

Daniel followed it, a series of crusty drops on the carpet that led down the hall. The crackle of a police radio in the living room made him turn. The local PD was still holding the three members of staff, lined up like guilty schoolchildren and looking at him with nervous eyes.

He passed them by without a word. Let them stew for a bit.

The blood trail continued, the dots getting smaller and more widely spaced as the murder weapon—a curved, sharp object from the initial analysis—began to run out of gore.

There was enough still dripping from it that when Daniel made it out to the deck, he could follow the trail straight to the pool. There the trail stopped and did not resume.

Cleaned his murder weapon. Hardly seems necessary at this point.

Daniel stood a moment next to the pool on a deck with a fabulous view of the Atlantic, thinking over this odd detail. The deck had not only a pool, but a wet bar and expensive sound system. The view was unobstructed because it was raised up. A flight of stairs took him down to ground level, where a narrow garden surrounding the deck was enclosed by a ten-foot wall topped with spikes of elaborate ironwork. Artistically done, but still pointy enough to hurt someone trying to climb over.

Unless you've brought along a short step ladder and a heavy tarpaulin you fold over several times and lay on top of the spikes. The murderer had left those behind.

Daniel shook his head. How many times had he seen rich people get robbed because they didn't take better security measures? They all thought their exclusive neighborhood would protect them. Well, Dyson had certainly learned different.

He climbed the step ladder, dusty from where CSI had checked for fingerprints and found none and peeked over the fence. Grass clung to sandy soil, quickly giving way to beach. In the near portion he could see a long, flattened area where the murderer had dragged something to obscure his tracks. Something about a yard wide. The trail ended at the high tide point.

Daniel got on his phone and checked the tide schedule for the local area. Yep, high tide was about an hour after estimated time of death. He'd bet a hundred bucks that hadn't been coincidental.

He climbed down off the ladder and looked it over. He found a small, sticky rectangular area with a bit of blown sand clinging to it. The killer had removed the price tag, of course. The guy thought of everything. At least he thought he thought of everything. No perp in the history of crime ever really did. They all slipped up somehow.

He went up the wooden steps back to the deck to find a member of the East Hampton police department waiting for him. A soft man, soft in the belly and soft in the eyes thanks to his cushy job. Not like the tough big-city cops Daniel had admired as a kid.

Not like Daniel either. He had a spare tire too, but his eyes were not soft. They hadn't been soft since he was twelve.

"You want to speak to the staff now?" the police officer asked. Daniel couldn't think of him as a "cop." That word implied gritty streets and strong-arming perps. Those guys had been the heroes of Daniel's childhood. If only he had summoned the strength to talk to one.

"Let them sweat it out for a bit," Daniel said. "Show me the security footage."

The officer shook its head. "It's a hell of a sight."

He led Daniel through the kitchen—bright lights, gleaming chrome, a bowl of exotic tropical fruit Daniel couldn't identify—to a little annex where a battery of CCTVs took up a portion of one wall.

"I already have it ready," the officer said.

The officer pushed a button. A camera showed the back deck from a high angle, obviously near the roof. In the lower righthand corner the time said 2:14 a.m. and today's date. The wall was at the limit of the frame. The silent image showed a pair of hands come into view and lay the tarp over the spikes.

Then a figure appeared, cowled like a medieval monk. It brought one leg over the wall, revealing light slacks and deck shoes, then straddled the fence.

The figure reached over to the far side of the wall (*lefthanded*) and pulled up a scythe of the kind farmers used to use.

The figure carefully set it down on the other side of the wall, then struggled back and forth a minute while gripping onto the top of the wall with both hands.

Daniel stared, unsure what he was doing.

That became clear a few second later when he lifted the ladder up with one foot.

Once he got it high enough to grab with his hands, he lifted it over the wall and set it down on the other side.

Idiot didn't bring a tall enough ladder.

The figure (*male, average build, approximately six feet tall)* grabbed the scythe and climbed partway up the stairs to the deck. He paused for a moment, looking at the house, then decided the coast was clear and moved quickly across the deck and out of sight.

Healthy. Calm. Confident.

"Huh," Daniel said. "Any footage from inside the house?"

"No cameras."

Daniel shook his head.

The police officer fast forwarded four and a half minutes to when the figure reappeared on camera.

Familiar with the layout of the house. No way he could have snuck in past three staff members and killed the guy and reemerged in that short of a time.

The figure carried a satchel containing a rectangular, bulky object. Obviously the painting (*approximately two feet by one and a half feet, that smaller bulge next to it must be the book*). The scythe dripped with blood. The killer dipped it into the pool, shook it clean, and hurried to the ladder without looking back.

A moment later he was over the fence and gone.

"That's it?" Daniel asked.

"That's it."

The medieval get up is part of the show. He wanted to tell something to his victim by dressing as the figure of death.

Tell something to us too. He knew the cameras were there. That's why he kept his head down, so the cowl would hide his features.

"Let's go talk to the staff," Daniel said.

They were still lined up in the living room under the watchful eye of another of East Hampton's finest. Another soft-eyed officer in uniform who was more accustomed to dealing with drunk drivers than murderers. The only difference from the first officer was that she was a woman.

The first staff member was an erect older man with jowls, a pot belly, and swept back receding gray hair. He was dressed as a butler. The second was thinner and younger and looked Italian or Italian-American. He was dressed as a chauffeur. The third was a woman who could not have been more than twenty. Blonde, buxom, with luscious lips and bright blue eyes. She was hardly dressed at all.

Daniel had already read through their initial statements on the way over.

He pointed at the butler. "You say you found him."

The butler nodded, seemingly unphased by what had happened to his master.

"Yes, sir," he said in a refined English accent. "I got up at six to prepare Mr. Dyson's breakfast. The cook prepares lunch and dinner. Mr. Dyson always has his breakfast at 6:30 a.m. sharp. My room is just off the kitchen, so I didn't notice anything amiss until I took the breakfast tray out of the kitchen and down the main hallway. I noticed the light to the East Gallery was on and the door was open. It was then that I noticed the bloodstains on the carpet. I hurried down the hallway and found Mr. Dyson. Then I called the police and woke up the other members of staff."

"What were you doing at two in the morning?" Daniel asked.

"I was sleeping, sir. Mr. Dyson said I could go to bed at midnight after I prepared him a snack. He had made a new acquisition and wished to study it. He often studied through the night when he made a purchase."

"We'll get back to that." Daniel turned to the chauffeur. "So where were you?"

"Sleeping," the man replied. American. Brooklyn accent. "The last I saw of Mr. Dyson was when I drove him out of the city—"

"Which city?"

"New York City."

"Go on."

"I dropped him off in the morning at around ten and was told to pick him up at Eleven Madison Park, that's a restaurant, at two after he had his lunch. It was strange that he didn't have me drive him around like usual. When I picked him up he had a new painting."

"What did it look like?"

"I didn't see. It was wrapped." The chauffeur said like it was obvious. "He often bought artwork in the city at various dealers or auction houses. It always made him so happy. He'd be talkative and upbeat all the way home. This time, though, he was really quiet. Not depressed, really, but thoughtful. Hardly said a word the whole way back."

Daniel turned back to the butler. "Did you see this painting?"

"Yes, sir, when I brought him his snack. He had hung it himself in the East Gallery, taking down the Bloemaert to make room. I didn't get much of a look at it. It was the figure of Death on a horse riding through the night sky."

Daniel felt a little shiver go down his spine.

The figure of Death. Like the guy who visited him a few hours later.

The killer knew what the painting showed. Probably knew he had just bought it too.

"I'll want to talk with you a bit more later," Daniel said. "The officer will give me your numbers. Here's mine."

He handed each of the two men a card. Both took it with their right hand.

Now Daniel turned to the young woman, who wore a wispy little black negligée like that was the most normal thing in the world to wear when your boss had just gotten murdered.

"Did you see this painting?"

She looked him right in the eye, sizing him up. Her eyes were bloodshot and puffy. She breathed in a little too deeply in order to emphasize her cleavage and said, "Is it OK if we speak alone?"

Not in this context, it sure as hell isn't.

He turned to the female police officer. "Come with us." Looking at the male police officer he said, "Stay here with them."

"My name's Rebecca. I have a lot to tell you. We can talk in the bedroom," the young woman suggested, walking too close next to Daniel for comfort.

"How about the West Gallery?" Daniel suggested, his voice coming out somewhat strangled. He'd had a hell of a dry spell since Veronica had left him.

Thank God for female police officers to keep me from temptation.

CHAPTER THREE

The West Gallery was much like the East Gallery, except it looked out over a vast front lawn with manicured bushes and a partial view of a mansion opposite. The walls were covered in exceptional examples of Japanese and Chinese art, and a few tables were set with Ming vases.

Odd he put the Eastern stuff in the West Gallery. East is West and West is East and never the twain will meet? He had a sense of humor. Well, a nerdy sense of humor.

The woman turned to face him, the female officer standing close behind.

"So how long have you worked for Mr. Dyson?" Daniel asked, trying not to notice how she kept moving her hips slightly from side to side.

"Three years," Rebecca answered.

Daniel studied her face a moment.

"How old are you?"

"Twenty-one."

"Were you of age when you started working for him?"

"Yes." She sounded irritated.

"Will your ID and employment records confirm that?"

"It's not what you think."

Daniel raised an eyebrow, trying not to look at the woman's cleavage.

"And what do I think?"

"We never slept together."

The doubt must have been obvious on Daniel's face, because she said, "He wanted company, someone to show off at dinners and art galleries."

Daniel gestured at her negligée. "Come on. You dress like that around the house, and he never put the moves on you?"

The female police officer frowned at him. He ignored her. This wasn't sexual harassment. This was legitimate questioning. Maybe the killer was a jealous lover or angry big brother. Unlikely considering the MO, but he needed to follow up everything.

The young woman's face softened. "He couldn't. He was impotent. Prostate cancer. They had to remove the prostate and he couldn't get it up anymore. It messed with his bladder too. Poor guy had to wear men's undergarments. That's what they call diapers for adults. He just wanted to look at me and show me off in public a little. I'm a trained massage therapist, so I'd give him daily messages, but he never tried anything with me. Just talked. He was a good guy. He even paid for me to go to design school."

Tears started rolling down those high cheekbones. Daniel's gut told him they were real.

Daniel softened his tone to match hers. "So you were only there for massages and to show off to his friends."

She shook her head. "He didn't have any friends. That was my job."

Daniel remembered the lack of any mention of him in the society pages.

"Tell me more."

"He was like a hermit or something. He'd go out, to museums and the opera and all that, and bring me with him, but he never met anyone. And no one ever came to visit the house."

The killer knew the house, though. Former employee? Family?

"What about family?"

"He has a sister in L.A. who he talked to sometimes on the phone. She's got a couple of kids. I know Monty sent them nice gifts. I'd help pick them out."

"Did they ever visit?"

"No. He'd go there a couple of times a year. He never brought me along for those trips."

"Did you see the painting?"

"Yeah. He was very excited about it. Not sure why. It gave me the creeps. It showed this thin old guy on a horse with a big sword. Looked like he was going to kill everybody in this little town below the horse."

"Did he say much about it?"

"No. Said he'd be studying it all night and that I should go to bed."

"Did he mention where he bought it?"

Her brow furrowed. "You know, that's kinda strange. He didn't. He would always say, 'Oh, I made a killing at Sotheby's,' or 'Look what I got from Antiquities International'. He knew all the dealers. It was his only social life, besides me, that is. He'd sit with them and have lunch and talk art, and then he'd buy something."

"Did they ever come here, or did he ever go to their homes?"

The young woman shook her head. "Never. He was pretty shy. Lost in his little world of finance and art. Outside of that he got real uncomfortable. He could only talk to the art dealers because they shared his passion. If some guy sitting next to us at the opera struck up a conversation at intermission, he'd get all awkward. I always had to do most of the talking."

"Are there any other staff members besides the cook and the two men I've already met?"

Daniel already knew the cook was a woman, so she wasn't the killer.

"A pool cleaner and garden crew come once a month or so."

"Do they ever come in the house?"

Rebecca shook her head. "Monty never let anyone in the house if he didn't have to."

"Any former employees have a problem with him? Male employees?"

"Not that I know. Antonio, the chauffeur, is new. Hired last year to replace a guy named Kevin who wanted to move to Chicago to get married. I don't know any other male employees. He must have had others over the years. Ask Winston. That's the butler."

Now we're getting somewhere. If Dyson had been such a hermit with no family, it had to have been an ex-employee.

"All right," Daniel said, leading the two women out of the room.

Going back to the living room where Winston and Antonio waited with the male police officer, Daniel went up to the butler.

"How long have you been working for Mr. Dyson?" he asked Winston.

"Eighteen years, sir," the butler said with a note of pride.

"Can you write me a list of all former male employees?"

"Certainly, sir. I can go through the records and give you their last known addresses and telephone numbers."

"That would be great. Are you familiar with the books in the East Gallery?"

"Yes, sir."

"One or two are missing. Go and try and figure out which."

"Yes, sir. Before I look through the employee records, sir?"

"Yes." Daniel turned to the driver. "Are you familiar with the East Gallery?"

"Not really."

"Go with him anyway."

They left. The male officer gave him a significant look. Daniel nodded and the policeman followed the butler and chauffeur.

Daniel sat in a comfortable old armchair, rubbing his temples and wondering why he was here. Sure, this murder involved the theft of some old painting, but that wasn't enough to attract the Antiquities Division of the FBI. He supposed it was because Dyson was rich. If he had been some middle-class slob who saved up to buy a nice painting, the FBI wouldn't have cared.

Closing his eyes, he settled into the armchair and cursed his luck. He should be back in the Behavioral Affairs Unit chasing serial killers. That was his true talent, not looking for some weirdo who scythed a billionaire to death. He'd been switched to the Antiquities Division as a demotion thanks to his habit of mouthing off to superiors and rough handling of suspects.

At least his first case with the new division had been a serial killer. Solved in record time thanks to an extremely useful and often annoying civilian advisor.

But getting a serial killer case in the Antiquities Division had been a fluke. There wouldn't be another one. This seemed like a pretty obvious case. Ex-employee or fellow art lover had a grudge against Dyson and came to kill him in a showoff sort of way. Maybe he got hurt financially by one of Dyson's business dealings. You couldn't make that much money without ripping someone else off.

God, why am I stuck with a case like this? The BAU needs me.

And I need the BAU.

"Are you all right?" Rebecca asked. Daniel had forgotten she and the female police officer were there.

Daniel opened his eyes.

Rebecca stood close to the armchair, too close. Daniel tried not to look at those legs within easy reach. Instead, he looked at her face and saw genuine concern there.

"You look upset," Rebecca said.

Just lost her sugar daddy and she's actually worried about me. No wonder Dyson chose her. She doesn't just have looks; she's got heart too.

"I'm fine," he said.

"You want me to make you some coffee or a sandwich or something?"

Daniel smiled. "No thanks."

A fantasy about her began to form in his mind. He pushed it away.

She's out of your league. Just because you're going through a divorce you can't start slobbering over every college girl who shows you a bit of kindness.

The look the female officer was giving him showed she agreed.

Fortunately, the two male servants returned just at that moment. The butler took a step closer to him.

"We keep a full list of every antiquarian book in the house, sir, and its location. The missing book is *A Map and Guide to the Heavens*, published in 1648."

Winston held out a spiral folder and pointed to a spot on the list.

"An astronomy book?" Daniel asked, standing up.

"So it would seem, sir. Members of staff were asked never to touch the antiquarian books or artwork. Mr. Dyson was quite particular on that point, sir. He would clean, hang, and arrange everything himself. It was his passion."

"Anything else missing?"

"Not that I could see, sir."

"Did he keep a list of paintings?"

"Yes, sir," he said, holding out another spiral bound volume of printouts. "He had not yet added his most recent acquisition."

"Where did he keep his receipts?"

"In his desk, sir, until the accountant goes over them."

"Show me his office."

The butler led him to a quiet office with a Persian rug and oak paneling. In the desk Daniel found a folder of recent receipts, including one for a nineteenth century Chinese snuffbox purchased at Christie's the week before and the receipt for lunch at Eleven Madison Park from the day before, but no receipt for a painting.

The butler looked puzzled. "It should be here."

The police had already given Daniel an itemized list of the objects on the victim's person, including the wallet that was still in his pocket. There had been no receipt in there either.

"Would it be unusual for him not to put his receipt in here?"

"Very unusual, sir. Mr. Dyson was a very methodical man. Perhaps Mr. Mitchell has it. He's Mr. Dyson's attorney. Mr. Dyson consulted him on major purchases. For such high expenditures and customs duties, it is best to have an attorney on hand for legal advice."

Daniel tapped his thumb against his thigh three times, glanced around the office, and said, "Let's go."

He led Winston back to the other staff members, then went alone to the East Gallery to take another look.

The room gave a beautiful, unobstructed view of the Atlantic, where the last shadows of evening were fading into the weak light of a new day. Out to sea he could see the distant lights of ships. He found himself wishing he was out there on one of them, sailing somewhere. Anywhere.

The sound of muffled footsteps on the Persian rug made him turn. The male police officer entered.

"I'm thinking," Daniel said.

The guy cocked his head, irritated.

"I said I'm thinking."

Eye contact, for half a second. Then the officer slumped a fraction of an inch, turned, and left.

Daniel took a look around at the paintings and could name most of the artists.

Giotto. Degas. Manet. Lots of big names. He didn't recognize any of the paintings, though. Must have always been in private hands.

"Works of art should be in public galleries," Uncle Ray said, walking with him through the Louvre, arm around thirteen-year-old Daniel's shoulder. "Beauty should be seen, admired, not hidden away."

Uncle Ray gave his shoulder a squeeze. Daniel blushed, not replying. He knew what Uncle Ray meant.

"Getting a bit tired?" Uncle Ray asked. "We've been here a couple of hours already."

"I'm fine. We can stay."

"Maybe we should go back to the hotel and ... rest for a while."

"No. I'd like to stay."

"Oh, but I'm tired too," Uncle Ray said.

Daniel's stomach turned.

"Just a couple more rooms?" he pleaded.

Uncle Ray chuckled. "An admirer of beauty! That's good. So am I. Let's go look at the Greek statues. An interesting culture, the Greeks. Let me tell you a bit about them ..."

Daniel shook himself, glanced around to make sure no one saw, then wiped his brow.

Focus on the present.

I can't with all this stuff reminding me.

Focus anyway. Want to get back to hunting serial killers? You need to crack a few cases in this junk division.

His gut told him the missing painting was bought illegally. That would explain the lack of a receipt and Dyson telling his chauffeur to get lost for the day. So this really was a job for the Antiquities Division. Stolen artwork was big business.

But he wasn't an expert on the art world. He'd been given this job because he had a strong educational background in art history and a bit of archaeology, but he didn't know much about the business of art.

At least he knew someone who did.

He pulled out his phone and smiled. It would be good to talk with her again. As irritating as she could be, Remi Laurent was good company.

CHAPTER FOUR

Remi and Cyril sat at Perla di Napoli, a lovely Italian restaurant near the university. Over the past few months, they had tried all the French restaurants in the area and Remi had found them all lacking. She had come to the conclusion that you could not get good French cuisine outside of France.

Luckily, America had enough of an Italian population that you could find several acceptable Italian options.

They sat in a quiet corner, a candle stuck in a chianti bottle between them. They clinked glasses and smiled as cheerful Italian music played through the sound system.

They took a sip of a rich Sicilian Nero d'Avola, enjoying its deep flavor and heady bouquet.

"Sooo," he said, leaning a little closer. "We need to think of a date."

He was referring to when they would get married. Cyril was divorced, and so he hadn't gotten on one knee, ring in hand, and proposed. Instead, he had discussed it with her a couple of months before in a practical, matter-of-fact manner as if he wanted to change a syllabus.

He had pointed out that they loved each other, got along well, and while the university frowned on relationships between professors, they didn't have a problem with those who were married. An odd quirk of the American educational system. In France, people did what nature demanded.

Cyril had reminded her that her work visa would expire in nine months. Cyril wanted her to stay and getting married would be the most practical solution.

Cyril was always practical.

At least for his own life.

What was she supposed to do for work? Georgetown didn't have the funds to turn her temporary position into a permanent one, and no other universities in the region were hiring. Cyril hadn't thought of that until Remi pointed it out.

And that set off alarm bells in her head. If he wasn't thinking about her career before they even got married, would he think about it even less after? And his businesslike handling of the proposal made it seem like she was a box being ticked off a to-do list.

But she loved him. While he could be a bit selfish and clingy, he had so many good traits too. Kind, affectionate, her intellectual equal, a wonderful father to the daughter he had with his first wife, and his volunteer work showed his selfishness didn't run too deep.

A flicker of impatience ran across Cyril's features and Remi realized she had paused a moment too long.

"Yes, a date. Um, I wanted to talk with you about that. I have a research trip to go on soon, and it would be better to get that out of the way first."

"A research trip?" Cyril said with surprise.

"Yes. To Florence. I'd only need a week. I need to look at the unpublished archaeological reports of a Tuscan church."

"Which article is this for?"

Currently she was working on two academic articles for leading journals, neither of them on churches.

"It's for a new line of inquiry. Well, actually an old one," she could feel herself babbling, fumbling. *Just come out and say it!*

"About what?" her lover asked. The wary note in his voice hinted that he was beginning to suspect.

Just then her phone rang. Usually she put it on silent when on a date with Cyril. Fortunately, this time she forgot.

She checked it, not looking at Cyril's face. She knew how it would look.

Her heart did a backflip when she saw it was FBI Agent Daniel Walker.

Why would he be calling? Some loose end with the cryptex case?

"Sorry," she said to Cyril, "It's the FBI. I have to take this."

Surprise and annoyance vied for prominence in her lover's expression. Annoyance looked like it was winning, so Remi turned away and lowered her voice.

"Hello Dan—Agent Walker. How are you this evening?"

"Good. Is this a bad time?"

"You didn't ask that when you burst into my class a few weeks ago," Remi said, covering her wry smile with her hand.

"Yeah, sorry about that," Daniel said in an offhand manner that told her he was anything but sorry. "Look, I've been dumped with a case that's a bit beyond me. It involves a stolen painting, a figure of one of the Four Horsemen of the Apocalypse. Death, to be exact. I have a feeling the painting the killer stole has been stolen before. I don't know much about the art market, and I could use your help. Can you come to Quantico tomorrow? I'm at the murder scene right now on Long Island but I'll be flying back on the evening flight."

"All right," she said without thinking.

Wait, what was she getting herself into?

"Oh wait," she corrected. "Tomorrow? I have a morning and afternoon lecture tomorrow."

"I'll write you a hall pass."

"A what?"

"I'll call your department head and tell him its FBI work. He'll have to say yes."

"Maybe call the dean like last time," she said. Her department head was sitting opposite her, wine in hand, trying to figure out what was going on.

"All right. I still have his number."

He kept the dean's number? Was he expecting to use me again?

That felt even more exciting, although Remi did not pursue just why she felt that way.

"How long will I be needed?" Remi asked.

"This is just an initial consultation. You might even be back in time for your afternoon lecture." Remi felt a sting of disappointment, quickly soothed by what Daniel said next. "But if you do come aboard, it might last a while. You can never tell with a case. I can't talk much about it over the phone, but the victim was an important person. We'll have all the resources we want for this one."

"I'll see you at your office at nine tomorrow morning. Text me the directions." Remi glanced at Cyril, who stared back at her, obviously impatient. "I really need to go now. Talk to you tomorrow."

"Looking forward to it! I mean, um, I really could use your input."

"Great. Until tomorrow."

She hung up, resisted the urge to do a little dance, took a deep breath, and turned to Cyril.

"It's the FBI, isn't it?"

Cyril's voice did not sound approving. Remi shifted in her seat.

"Yes," she said, looking down at her food.

"What do they want? Are there loose ends in the case or something?"

"Um, no. It's a … new case."

"A new case!" Everyone in the restaurant turned to look. Cyril gave an embarrassed glance around, learned forward and in a harsh whisper said, "A new case? What do you mean a new case?"

"It seems someone was murdered over a stolen painting. They need my help."

Remi swelled with pride.

"How is that your business?" Cyril demanded. "You're a university professor for Christ's sake!"

"Don't make a scene. Agent Walker needs my help as a consultant."

"They can get another historian. You nearly got killed last time."

"Don't exaggerate."

Actually, Cyril was saying more than he knew. Remi hadn't told him how close to death she had come.

"This isn't your job, Remi. You're not a policeman."

"They need me."

"The department needs you. I need you. And it looks bad if you go gallivanting off on another case when you should be teaching your students."

Remi crossed her arms and frowned. "It looks bad for who, me or you?"

"Both of us. Look, you had your fun with your little case. You caught that horrible man and did some good for the world. Now try and be more sensible."

Little case? Little case! She helped track down a serial killer who had murdered at least half a dozen people. She had discovered one of the most sought-after artifacts in history. And he calls that a little case?

Remi grabbed her purse and got up.

"Where are you going?" Cyril asked.

"Home. I have to get up early tomorrow. Quantico is an hour's drive away and I have an appointment at nine."

"But—"

Remi ignored him, turning her back on him and nearly colliding with a waiter, who was just approaching their table with their dinner.

Remi ducked past him and hurried out the door.

She had another “little case” to solve. And her partner at the FBI, despite being uncouth, had more respect for her abilities than the man she had left sitting alone in the restaurant.

CHAPTER FIVE

The next morning, Remi drove down to Quantico, Virginia, to meet Daniel at the FBI headquarters. She spent the first half of the one-hour drive fuming over Cyril's behavior. How could he belittle the most terrifying, most rewarding experience of her life? And who was he to think that he could tell her what to do?

If he was this controlling now, how would he be once they were married?

That question had bothered her all last night, and she had woken up still angry.

And yet she couldn't help but feel a bit guilty too. Cyril had wanted to discuss wedding arrangements, and the first thing she did was put him off with a proposed research trip. Then, a moment later, she left in a huff without even staying for dinner.

While he had been too overbearing, she had overreacted. She'd call him later, once she knew more about this case. It could be that they only wanted her to look over a few files and that she would be back for her afternoon lecture, as Daniel had suggested.

That would be a disappointment. She wanted a challenging case, something exciting. Perhaps not a knife-wielding religious maniac with a strange fixation for her, one of those was quite enough for one lifetime, but at least something to pull her out of her dull daily life.

She spent the second half of the drive considering her options. On the last case, Daniel had told her about the Antiquities Division. It covered much the same ground as her research area and, being a new and underfunded division, it was somewhat understaffed. She sensed Daniel felt he had been demoted when they transferred him there. That made her wonder what sort of cases he had been handling in the Behavioral Affairs Unit.

He had made no mention of the Antiquities Division having a historian on staff. While they weren't going to hire her to be an FBI agent, and she didn't want to give up academia, it would be wonderful to have some sort of permanent status as a consultant. They had paid fairly well for the last case, and perhaps being on the FBI payroll would allow her both the money and the visa to stay after her visiting lectureship ended in nine months.

That would take the pressure off in so many ways. The Sorbonne would be amenable to her staying on in the United States for a while (some of the old men running the department were happy to have her on the other side of the Atlantic) and there wouldn't be a ticking clock for her and Cyril's marriage plans.

That had been going too fast. If she could get a job as a consultant for the new division, their relationship could proceed at its proper pace.

If she could get the job. She didn't even know if it was possible.

And what would that mean for her academic career? If she didn't keep going to conferences, didn't keep up a regular pace of publishing, she'd sink into obscurity. After a while, it would be impossible to get back into the system. Did she really want to give all that up?

She didn't have an answer to that. The priority at the moment was finding out more about this case.

As she pulled into the parking lot location that Daniel had sent to her GPS, she found him standing there. She waved, pulled into a free space, and eagerly stepped out of her car.

Daniel Walker looked the same as she remembered—a tall man about her age with broad shoulders who would have looked athletic if it wasn't for a sizeable gut. He wore his usual black suit and tie. She had never seen him wear anything else. A handsome face with short brown hair and intelligent brown eyes looked more rested than when she had last seen him.

His face cracked into a smile. Daniel looked much better when he smiled. He didn't do it very often.

They shook hands warmly.

"Glad to have you on board," he said. "How have things been at Georgetown?"

"Good. I've been following some interesting research."

To put it mildly.

Remi hadn't told Daniel that she had sneaked a peek inside the cryptex. Since it had been museum property, her handling it was technically illegal. While Daniel often bent the rules, she had decided not to bring it up.

"Sounds nice," Daniel said, leading her toward a large office building. "Let's go to my office and look over the material I have. I need to fly to New York City today to grill the art dealers. Also need to talk to the victim's attorney. I'd love your input before I go."

"Wait, if the murder was on Long Island, why didn't you go straight to New York City?"

"Because I needed to speak with you. Better in person than on the phone. And the boss needed to talk with me about the case too. One thing I had to get used to in the FBI was flying back and forth all the time."

While she felt good that part of the reason he had come back was to speak with her, Remi felt a tug of regret to hear she hadn't been invited to go to New York. She had hoped to be swept up into another exciting chase like last time. She had even packed a suitcase just in case.

Subdued, she passed through security, was given a temporary visitor's pass, and Daniel escorted her to a tiny office with his name on the door. There was little room for anything other than a couple of chairs, a desk, and a computer. A small window looked out on the bare concrete wall of the neighboring building.

"Home sweet home," Daniel said with an abashed smile.

"So tell me what you know so far," she said, eager to get started.

Daniel ran through the particulars of the murder of Montgomery Dyson, a billionaire art collector she had never heard of. He showed her security footage of a man dressed like death breaking into the property then coming out shortly thereafter and washing his scythe in the pool. Remi felt a prickle of disgust and, she had to admit, excitement.

Next, he showed her photos of the crime scene, a private gallery in the billionaire's home.

"This is horrible! Shocking!" Remi cried.

"What?" Daniel said, looking at the gallery of photos. "I thought I took out all the photos of the victim."

"It's not that; it's the setup of this gallery. Look, a window overlooking the sea, and it's even open. A salty breeze is blowing on these paintings all day. They've survived centuries thanks to proper care and now they'll be ruined within a few decades. *Sacre bleu!* The Degas is even warped a bit on the corner closest to the window. This man is a criminal! *Grossier! Classe inférieure!*"

"Go easy. The guy got hacked to death in his own home with a scythe."

"Well, I suppose he didn't deserve that, but what he did to these works of art is unforgiveable."

Daniel burst out laughing.

"What?" Remi asked, confused.

Daniel wiped his eyes, still laughing.

"What?"

The FBI agent shook his head. "Oh, I've missed you. You're hilarious."

Remi smiled. "I've … missed this too."

Daniel paused for the briefest of moments. Remi tensed.

"So what do you think?" he asked. "Besides the fact that Dyson was an American peasant who should have never owned any art."

"He most certainly was a peasant. Perhaps the wealthiest peasant in the world. It's interesting that a rare book on astronomy was stolen."

"Are you familiar with that book?"

"No. It's a bit late for my period of study, although of course I've studied medieval and Renaissance ideas of cosmology."

"Of course, who hasn't?"

Remi suspected that was sarcasm and decided to ignore it. She was too intrigued by the subject to care.

"So you say the painting was a figure of death riding in the sky over a village, with a manor house in the lower righthand corner?"

"That's what the butler said. The trophy girl was more vague but gave the same general description."

"Night sky?"

"Yeah. Does Death ever ride into town during the day?"

"Not generally, no. And there were no other paintings of the Four Horsemen in the house?"

"No. Oh wait, there was an engraving by Dürer, the famous one of the four horsemen. In the same room. Do you know the painting that got stolen?"

"I might," Remi mused. "The Four Horsemen of the Apocalypse was a common theme, but we can narrow it down thanks to the dimensions, approximate period, and the fact that it was in private hands."

"I already checked the stolen art international database," Daniel said. "It's not on it."

"When do records start for that database?"

"What? Oh, I see what you mean. The database was set up around thirty years ago. There are some older records on there, especially for art stolen by the Nazis. But if it was stolen before the 21st century, there's a decent chance it isn't on there."

"Hmmm."

Remi pulled out her phone and started to type.

Daniel tut-tutted. "Just like your students. Can't concentrate for more than fifteen minutes before needing to text your friends."

"I am texting a friend," Remi said with a smile. "Her name is Eleah Smets, an art curator in Brussels. She has consulted with the European Union on stolen artwork."

"Is she single?"

"Don't be gauche. You have a wife."

"Not anymore."

Remi looked up, shocked.

"I-I'm sorry."

Daniel waved a dismissive hand. "I'm not. Continue with your email."

Remi didn't believe his cavalier attitude to getting divorced. It was so typical of this man to shrug off any feelings and not discuss them. She had caught him several times, when he thought he was unobserved, brooding over something. As soon as he noticed someone else nearby, he'd put on a neutral mask.

This divorce must have really eaten at him. But she knew he wouldn't speak of it. After all, they weren't even friends, just temporary colleagues.

Getting back to the case, she explained the situation to Eleah Smets and asked if she knew of any such painting in private hands. Eleah had her finger on the pulse of the art trade, both legitimate and illegal. If anyonc would know, it would bc hcr.

"Hopefully she'll get back to me soon," Remi said, putting her phone away.

"She sounds like a useful informant. Thanks for that. You'll have to give me her contact info."

"She's too busy to work for the FBI."

"Don't worry," Daniel said. "If I hire anyone, I'll hire you."

That felt satisfying. Even more than that, it felt *right*, like she belonged.

Remi took a deep breath and plunged in. "I've been thinking … the Antiquities Division is a new branch of the FBI, and you don't have anyone who is a specialist in antiquities. You have a great deal of knowledge yourself—" Daniel's face hardened. Why? Why the resistance to the past? "—but you could use someone who is deeper into the material. I think it would be more useful for the division to have a civilian expert retained as a consultant on a more permanent basis."

"You want to work for the FBI?" Daniel looked surprised.

"Not as an employee per se. I don't think they'd hire me."

"They wouldn't. You have to go through the academy."

"I understand. But I've been hired as a civilian consultant before. And for at least today I have been hired again. Why not make that something more long term?"

"Getting tired of teaching bored undergrads?"

"That's part of it," Remi admitted.

Daniel thought a moment. Remi sat on the edge of her seat.

"It's possible," he said at last. "It's been done before. But I'm not the one to make that call. You'll need to see my boss."

"Can we go now?"

"We need to get going on this case," Daniel said, sounding impatient.

"This will help," Remi said. A slow smile spread across her face. "It will help with the next case too."

Daniel broke into a smile.

"All right, we'll try. Don't get your hopes up, though."

CHAPTER SIX

Keiko Ochiai, Assistant Director of the Antiquities Division, was not what Remi had expected.

She had imagined Daniel's boss to be some square-jawed older man who looked like a marine and swore like a sailor.

Instead she found herself talking to an immaculately dressed Japanese-American woman. She didn't look any older than Remi, which meant that she was just as devoted to, and successful in, her line of work as Remi was to hers.

They sat in comfortable chairs in a spacious corner office. A large window overlooked a garden. Artful black and white photos on the walls showed horses and cattle and Asian ranch hands.

"I want to congratulate you on your fine work with the Cryptex Killer case," Assistant Director Ochiai said in a surprising Texas drawl. "And thank you for helping with this one too. Montgomery Dyson isn't your usual murder victim. He was on the Fortune 500. His cousin is the senior senator from Pennsylvania."

"I see," Remi said. "I'll be available for the entire case if you need me."

"Agent Walker is flying to New York this afternoon. I can approve travel funds for you to go with him. I'm sure you have already packed a suitcase."

Remi blinked. This woman was a good judge of character.

"I have."

Out of the corner of her eye she saw Daniel turn to stare at her.

"Excellent," Assistant Director Ochiai said. "You'll be a great asset to Agent Walker."

"So you want me to be on the case for more than an initial consultation?" She hadn't even had the chance to ask. This was going better than she had hoped.

"Certainly. If you have the time."

"I can make the time." Remi licked her lips, cleared her throat, and went on. "I was thinking that I could be more of an asset to Agent

Walker, and to Antiquities Division, if I was a consultant on a more permanent basis."

Assistant Director Ochiai cocked her head. "Meaning?"

"If I could be brought on board as a long-term civilian consultant, I would be on hand to help Agent Walker with cases, as well as other problems that come across your desk. My father was a police officer in Paris, and he always complained there were far more leads to follow up than personnel to handle them. I don't suppose it's any different in America."

"It sure isn't. But wouldn't your obligations at Georgetown University keep you too busy for this sort of work?"

"My visa expires in nine months. After that I will have to return to France."

"Are you suggesting you stay on in the United States longer than that?"

"I'd be willing, as long as my wage was sufficient."

Assistant Director Ochiai studied her for a long moment. Remi tensed. She would not want to be under that piercing gaze in an interrogation room.

"Eager for a change of career, eh? Taking you on board on a semi-permanent basis would be no simple matter. It has to go through channels and get approval from people higher up the chain of command. Doing well on one single case might not be enough to convince them."

Probably not. But is this even what I want? This would be such a big change. All that work in graduate school, all that climbing up the academic ladder ...

I can decide later, assuming they even make the offer.

Remi looked her in the eye. It was no easy thing to do. "I'll do well on this case too."

Was that a spark of approval she saw in the assistant director's eyes?

If so, it didn't come out in her voice.

"We'll see. And even then, it's no guarantee. But we do appreciate your help, Professor Laurent."

Remi felt uncertain about her next request but decided to plunge ahead.

"There's a certain amount of danger in these cases. The little bottle of pepper spray I carry in my purse isn't enough to protect me. Could I get a permit to carry a concealed firearm?"

Beside her, Daniel sputtered.

Assistant Director Ochiai shook her head. "No."

"I need—"

"No. You're on an H1 visa. You're not allowed to bear arms. Not even the director of the FBI could clear that with Customs and Immigration, unless you were a foreign police officer working on a special case on U.S. soil. Which you're not. Even then it's difficult."

"But last time—"

"No. If you become a permanent resident, it's possible, but not with your current status. You are a civilian consultant, Professor Laurent, not an officer of the law. Now I'm sure you and Agent Walker have a lot to do before your flight."

Having been essentially told the meeting was over, Remi and Daniel stood.

Remi didn't want to leave the office on a sour note, though. She smiled and pointed to the photos.

"These are well done," Remi said. "Who took them?"

Assistant Director Ochiai smiled. "I did. A hobby of mine."

"She won the FBI photography contest three years in a row," Daniel told her.

"And Agent Walker won the marksmanship award two years running. You won't need a gun with him at your side, Professor Laurent."

* * *

Daniel let out a gust of relief as they left the building. That had gone better than any meeting he had ever had with Assistant Director Ochiai. Maybe she gave Remi the benefit of the doubt because she was a woman. Ochiai sure as hell didn't give him the benefit of the doubt.

"What's this about wanting a gun?" Daniel asked, slightly irritated that she hadn't told him that before. It made them both look ridiculous.

"I nearly got killed by the Cryptex Killer."

"Because you didn't listen to me when I told you to hang back."

"What if this killer springs on us by surprise? I need to be able to defend myself."

"You can't just pick up a gun and expect to be able to handle it. That takes training. Practice."

Remi shrugged. "Show me, then."

Daniel stared at her. "Show you?"

"Doesn't the FBI have a firing range?"

He clicked his tongue. "I can't take you there. Members only."

"You make it sound like an exclusive country club."

"Yeah, except with no golf course and no waiters. There's nothing exclusive about the FBI. Except for the fact that they don't allow civilians onto the firing range. Way too much liability."

Remi got on her phone.

"Did you get an answer from your Belgian friend?" Daniel asked.

"No, I'm looking for shooting ranges."

"Huh?"

"I need to practice." Her eyes widened. "Oh my! So many."

"Welcome to America. We don't have time for this. How about we solve the case and then I take you shooting."

Remi gave him that slightly superior, slightly amused look she used way too often. "How about I take myself shooting?"

"Because I can give you good advice. Anyway, back to the job. We're taking the next flight to New York, so I'm glad you have your bags packed and ready. We need to speak to a number of art dealers, at least one of whom is probably dealing in stolen art."

"Probably more than one. It's far too common."

"So I've heard. We need to trace the paintings. I think the best thing to do is for me to pretend to be a buyer and you're my assistant."

Remi arched an eyebrow. "Assistant?"

"Come on, it's just playacting. And it's for the case. You're my hired expert. Sound better?"

"Sounds accurate. But I don't think you would be convincing as a billionaire."

"No, perhaps not. We'll have to think of some other role." Daniel turned and looked her in the eye. "But we're playing in earnest, Remi. One of these art dealers may very well be the murderer. I need you to promise to stay close where I can protect you. You're not getting a gun, not now and probably not ever. You need to stick with me, work with me. Law enforcement uses the partner system for a reason. We guard each other's backs."

Still that arrogant smile. "All right, Daniel. I'll guard your back."

Daniel groaned inwardly. This woman was going to get them in trouble. Again.

He just knew it.

CHAPTER SEVEN

Remi had never liked New York City. She had found it too enclosed, too busy. It lacked the wide boulevards and ornate architecture of Paris.

And then there was that horrible accent—nasal, brash, even worse than the usual American accent.

But she couldn't deny there was a certain energy to this place that many other American cities lacked. The people here, instead of being sealed in their cars, were crammed together on bustling sidewalks. The smell of cooking and the shouts of street hustlers filled her senses. A black man in a Tupac t-shirt started rapping at them while waving his homemade CDs over his head, hoping for a sale.

They were in lower Manhattan, a place of giant high rises and giant fortunes. Their first stop in the city was to see Frederick Mitchell, who had served as Montgomery Dyson's attorney for the past fifteen years. A liveried doorman opened the door for them, and they found themselves in a gleaming foyer of marble and mirrors. A man in a suit at a front desk took their names and gave them directions to the 35th floor.

As they went up the elevator, Daniel turned to her and said, "Give me the info on that painting again."

Remi's Belgian friend had confirmed what she had suspected: that the painting was stolen.

"The painting was done by a minor 17th century Flemish artist named Jacob van der Veer. It was reported stolen in 1923 and has not been seen since. There's only one photo known of it."

Remi brought up the photo on her phone. While the photo wasn't of the best quality, it showed Death riding through the night sky. A village and larger house could be seen in the landscape below. The painter had emphasized the night sky, and even in the grainy, secondhand black and white photo, the stars showed up clearly. Death's scythe framed a constellation that Remi reminded herself to look up.

“Looks like Death is heading for that big house in the corner,” Daniel said. “A rich man’s house. I’m thinking our killer wanted to recreate the painting before he stole it.”

Remi felt a prickle of fear. Growing up with her father, she was accustomed enough to tales of murder. This, however, went a step beyond. It wasn’t just a crime of passion where an enraged husband picked up a knife against his wife and her lover, or some gang member shooting another over drug turf. No, this was preplanned, dramatized, and probably unnecessary. The police report said Dyson was an older man and not in the best of health. The younger man who appeared to have little problem climbing over a fence and wielding a heavy farm implement would have had no trouble subduing the billionaire if he had wanted to.

But he hadn’t wanted to. He wanted to cut Dyson down as the figure of Death itself.

“Send that to me,” Daniel told her. “I’ll forward it to the East Hampton police and see if Dyson’s staff can confirm it’s the same artwork.”

Just as she did so, the elevator pinged. They emerged into a quiet, corporate hallway and padded along thick carpet to an oak door bearing the attorney’s name on a plate of burnished brass.

The reception room was of subdued tones, the walls decorated with photos of yachts moored off some glittering Caribbean island. Remi wondered which of those yachts were Mitchell’s. Probably the biggest one.

An attractive woman in her thirties sat behind a desk. Daniel showed her his FBI identification. She did not seem phased, treating them both to a professional smile that lacked depth.

“Mr. Mitchell is expecting you. Go right in.”

They passed through another oak door and into a large office. Mitchell rose from the desk, a healthy, robust-looking man in his fifties with a fresh tan that showed he had been on his yacht down by that island recently. Behind him, a floor to ceiling window offered a breathtaking view of Manhattan.

“Thank you for coming,” he said, his face somber. “Such a tragedy.”

He shook Daniel’s hand, and then hers.

“Sit. Would you like me to get you coffee? Tea?”

Remi felt a mixture of amusement and irritation at this offer. He made it sound like he would be the one to prepare it, and not the woman outside.

"No, thank you," they replied.

They sat. Mitchell leaned back in a spacious leather chair and studied them a moment.

"How may I help you?"

"First off," Daniel said, "we'd like to know the details of Mr. Dyson's will."

"Certainly," the attorney said, pulling a thick set of papers out of a folder. "Although I'm afraid you won't find a suspect that way. The details of the will were kept in strictest confidence between Mr. Dyson and myself."

Daniel glanced through the pages. "Who are the main beneficiaries?"

"It is complicated, isn't it?" the lawyer said in a voice that sounded slightly condescending. "Fifty-three pages. A large portion goes to his sister, his only close relative, as well as a trust for her two children. Other assets go to various charities. There's also a generous payment to each member of his staff."

"What about Rebecca Holsen?" Daniel asked.

Remi remembered Daniel mentioning her.

Mitchell chuckled, glanced at Remi and said to Daniel. "Well, an extra generous portion to her. For services rendered, eh?" He tapped the side of his nose.

Pig.

"So no one knows of the terms of this will?" Daniel asked.

"No one. Well, now it's going through the process, but at the time of his murder"—Mitchell made a little shudder. Remi could not tell if it was genuine or not—"no one did. He told me several times that he never revealed it to anyone. Not even little Rebecca." Pause. Mitchell looked off into space. "I should give her a call. Not just about the good news, but to comfort her for her loss. Yes. I should definitely call her today."

Remi noticed a photo on the desk of Mitchell with a wife and two children.

"While I suppose you'll need to tell the beneficiaries," Daniel said, "I'd appreciate you not mentioning Mr. Dyson's death to anyone else. I've found that in murder investigations, the fewer people who know, the less chance the knowledge will compromise the investigation. People change when they hear someone has been murdered. Even if they aren't the culprit, they often get tight-lipped and defensive."

The attorney smiled. "It's the same with managing a will. Once word gets out, you get inundated with calls from people who think they should be beneficiaries or who claim the deceased owed them money. Don't worry, Mr. Walker, I haven't told anyone I haven't absolutely needed to tell."

Now it was time for Remi's part of the discussion. She leaned forward a bit to get his attention. So far, he had only been addressing Daniel.

"The motive for the killing was to steal a painting Mr. Dyson had purchased just that same day," she said. "We know he consulted you on the terms of major purchases, and we were wondering if he spoke to you about this painting. He seemed very excited about it."

Mitchell smiled. It came out flat. "Mr. Dyson was a connoisseur of the arts. I don't know much about that, I'm afraid. I'm more of an outdoorsman."

"But you helped him to purchase art, to get the art through customs and arrange the legal details of the deal. Some of the paintings in his personal gallery are worth millions. He would have needed you."

Mitchell looked away for a moment before remembering himself and retaining eye contact. "Oh, certainly. I helped arrange purchases once or twice."

"Did you help with this most recent painting? It was a 17th century Dutch piece showing one of the Four Horsemen of the Apocalypse. Death."

Another of those flat smiles. "I'm afraid that comes under attorney/client privilege."

"You showed us the will," Remi said, her irritation growing.

"That's becoming public. There are more than twenty individuals and institutions named as beneficiaries. It's hardly a private matter at this point. Mr. Dyson's purchases, however, are of a more private nature."

"This is a murder investigation," Daniel snapped.

Mitchell nodded. "I am fully aware of that. I am also aware that if you wish to see those records, you need to go through the proper channels."

"You mean a warrant?" Daniel said. "Sure, we can do that. Then we can go through every record, every receipt. What will we find there, Mitchell? You sure everything is aboveboard? Because we know that painting circulated on the stolen art market. You want to be brought up as an accessory to that?"

"I have no knowledge—"

"Yeah sure, you don't. And really, does it matter if you did or not? Think what the papers will say about it. They're already going crazy about the murder. If your name gets involved …"

Mitchell leaned back in his chair, looking unsettled for the first time in the interview.

"We just want to know about the painting," Remi said in a soothing voice. "We're concerned about catching the murderer. That's all. If you can help us with that, we don't need to look into all these other matters."

Mitchell stared at her as if seeing her for the first time.

"Are you FBI?"

"I'm a civilian consultant for the FBI."

His eyes flicked to Daniel and, seeing no help there, sized up Remi again.

"What sort of consultant?"

"Investigating art theft and bringing to justice those who steal it."

"You're an academic."

Less and less each day, it feels.

"When I'm not gathering evidence for arrests, yes I am."

Mitchell thought for a moment and said, "I didn't know the piece was stolen, but the dealer who sold it to him has a rather unsavory reputation. I could give you his contact information if …"

Remi glanced at Daniel, who didn't speak.

Do I have the authority to make deals like this?

Well, he isn't stopping me.

"We just want to bring the killer to justice, Mr. Mitchell," she said. "This will help speed up our investigation. We aren't concerned about investigating anything else."

The lawyer relaxed a little. "Very well, his name is Azad Sahakian. An Armenian immigrant with ties to the old country. He made his fortune in the '90s selling Soviet art when that was a boom after the Berlin Wall fell. Now he deals mostly in fine art and antiquities." Mitchell started tapping away on his computer. "Let me find his information for you. But I warn you, he's a very slippery character. It won't be easy to get any information from him."

As Mitchell occupied himself with his computer Daniel flashed her an approving smile.

Remi flushed with pride. She had just negotiated her first deal for the Federal Bureau of Investigation.

I really do have a talent for this. Now that I've dealt with a shady attorney, let's see how I deal with a shady art dealer.

CHAPTER EIGHT

Remi sat on a park bench with Daniel eating a horrible American invention—hotdogs. She found the bread too white and too spongey, and the wiener tasted like it was made of carcinogens mixed with plastic. How could Americans eat these things? Daniel had already eaten two, slathered in ketchup, mustard, and relish, and he was considering going back to the little cart on the street corner for a third.

Eating like a pig didn't stop him from doing his job, however. He was on the phone to the FBI asking about Azad Sahakian, the art dealer Mitchell had named. The agent waited a couple of minutes as they looked him up on the crime database.

"Yeah? Uh-huh?" Daniel said, nodding. Remi watched him, curious. "Really? OK, send over the files. Thanks."

He hung up and turned to her. "Just as we suspected, Sahakian is dirty. Well-known for dealing in stolen art. That explains why Dyson was sneaking around without his driver and why there wasn't a receipt. Sahakian has been brought up on charges twice but wriggled out both times. He's got a good lawyer, so we'll have to watch our step."

"Perhaps he wanted to steal the artwork back after selling it," Remi suggested.

"Maybe. I don't think so, though. He makes a good living selling art, so why run the risk? Especially with such a high-profile customer. He could probably make more keeping him on as a regular buyer."

"But the killer knew Dyson had just bought the Jacob van der Veer painting that same day. Who else would know besides Sahakian?"

"Maybe he sells information as well as art."

Remi thought about this a moment. That could fit.

"So another potential buyer, one who was desperate enough to get the painting that he would kill for it," Remi mused, "or offered Sahakian enough for the dealer to kill for it in order to retrieve it."

"But why the showmanship?" Daniel asked. "Why dress up like Death?"

"To steer us down the wrong path? Make us think we are dealing with an unhinged mind?"

"Maybe. More likely we really are dealing with an unhinged mind. When sane people try to shift blame, they do all the standard movie things like make it look like a Mafia hit or jealous lover or something. This is too theatrical."

Remi shook her head, frustrated. "I need to learn more about policework. My father was a regular patrol officer, walking the streets of Paris and responding to calls. He didn't conduct investigations. I learned a great deal about drug dealing and drunken brawls, but not much about the mind of a murderer. And I'm afraid my historical background isn't being all that much help on this case."

"We wouldn't have gotten this far if it wasn't for you. You identified the painting, after all. And got Mitchell to talk."

"That's all I've done," Remi said, staring at her inedible hotdog. Why did she think she could be brought on to work for the FBI full time? A silly fantasy. She was a professor and that's what she would probably be for life.

Daniel nudged her. "Don't be so glum. And don't be so impatient. These things take time. You cracked the last case, and I have a feeling you're going to be instrumental in this one."

Remi smiled. "You think so?"

"I wouldn't have requested you otherwise. And your knowledge will come in handy for our next step. We're going to Sahakian's gallery and pose as buyers."

"How do we do that?" she asked, surprised.

Daniel shrugged. "Simply walk in there, take a look around, and pretend we know what we're doing. That's where you come in. We'll bring him around to talking about the Van der Veer painting and see how he reacts. But slowly. We have to get his confidence first."

"I don't know how to pose as a billionaire."

"You're French. You all act upper class."

Remi clicked her tongue. "You never met some of the French people my father did."

"Good point, but somehow I think you had better people around you growing up, or did you deal crack in high school? No? Didn't think so. Here's what we do. We're buyers for a rich client. You're the art expert and I'm the bodyguard. I'll act like I'm carrying the cash and have come along to guard the painting once we make a purchase."

"That should work," Remi said, her heart beating faster. "Let's stop off at the hotel. I have a better dress and some jewelry I can put on. It won't be enough to play the role, but it will help."

Could she manage it? Acting wasn't one of her talents. The last time she had played a role she had been on stage in high school. In school plays, she was always given some minor role as the more extroverted boys and girls got the leads. And now she had to play a role in front of someone who might very well be a murderer, or in league with one.

She felt in over her head, and that worried and exhilarated her in equal measure.

* * *

Azad Sahakian's gallery was on a second-story walkup in an old brick building on the lower east side. From what Remi had seen in movies, this part of New York had been a rough area thirty years ago, full of punk rock venues and cheap bars, but had now been thoroughly gentrified. Everyone looked healthy and prosperous. Lots of designer labels and vacation suntans. The ground floor of the building housed an antique shop featuring Colonial furniture. A chic café, almost as good as the ones in Paris, stood next door, alongside a couple of high-end boutiques.

Sahakian buzzed them up without question and waited for them at the top of the stairs as they ascended. Remi saw a short, squat Armenian man with salt and pepper hair, a broad face, and more muscles than any art dealer she had ever met. In that part of the world, men all prided themselves on their physical strength.

"Welcome to Sahakian Art and Antiquities. How may I help you?" Sahakian's voice carried only the slightest accent. He had obviously lived in the United States for some time.

Remi decided to take the lead. "We're here for our employer. Just browsing at the moment."

"Certainly," Azad Sahakian said ushering them in. "Are you looking for any period in particular?"

Remi didn't answer at once. She scanned the room, a high-ceilinged place with tall windows that had probably once been a warehouse. Paintings of various periods hung on the walls, and in Perspex display cases were various ancient artifacts. Remi noted that the majority came from Iraq or Afghanistan. A little clay Sumerian votive figure of a man in a wool skirt, hands clasped in prayer, took a place of pride. Remi could not even estimate what such a museum-quality piece would cost. Nearby was a stack of glazed bricks imprinted with cuneiform, probably bearing the name of the king who commissioned the building. Another display case contained a bronze Buddha, the pose and clothing looking Greek rather than Eastern. This hailed from the civilization of Gandhara, which thrived in Afghanistan two thousand years ago and was an heir to the conquests of Alexander the Great.

Iraq ... Afghanistan ... two of the largest sources of illegal antiquities. And here he is showing them off to members of the public.

A small sign on the wall read, "Sahakian Art and Antiquities takes its obligation to international law seriously. Customers can be confident that all are antiquities are fully documented and sold with strict adherence to international antiquities regulations."

Remi just barely managed not to scoff.

"This is a fine piece," Sahakian said, coming up next to her and gesturing at the Buddha. "Is your employer interested in archaeological artifacts?"

"He's more interested in Early Modern painting. Especially from the Low Countries."

"Always a solid choice for investment," Sahakian said with a nod.

"Oh, he doesn't look at his collection as an investment, more as a field of study. He has a great interest in the symbolism that goes into paintings."

"Then perhaps he'd be interested in some alchemical prints from the 17th century?"

"He would be. Could we see them?"

While that wasn't the right medium, it was the right century and perhaps the right general theme. Flemish painters of that century often put alchemical symbolism in their paintings, and she was beginning to suspect the painting of Death might contain some symbolism Dyson had been interested in. Remi decided to play along, seeing where it might lead her.

Sahakian led her to a bureau with several wide shelves. Opening one up, he started to bring out 17th century engravings richly decorated with allegorical figures.

"Here's one from by Michael Maier from the *Tripus Aureus* of 1618."

"The Golden Tripod?" Remi asked, remembering her Latin.

"That's right. It was a collection of three alchemical treatises. Here you see two virgins riding lions confronting each other. Both carry hearts in their hands from which sprout a sun and a moon. This represents the purity and balance required to make true mixtures. The figure of the knight with his sword upraised on the edge of the print symbolizes—"

"Do you have anything with more astronomical and astrological symbolism?" Remi asked, staving off a lecture. "Our client is especially interested in such representations from the period. He's a student of such symbolism."

Sahakian didn't bat an eyelid. He put away the print and opened up another drawer.

"Here we have some excellent maps of the night sky. Note the quality of the figures representing the constellations."

"These are very nice," Remi agreed. "Did you have anything with a bit more of a religious bent, anything relating to the Book of Revelation?"

"I think I have a woodcut from the 14th century. I'll have to look in the back."

Daniel cut in. "That sounds like something he'd be interested in. Let's see."

"One moment," the art dealer said when Daniel tried to follow him. The agent gave her a rueful look as Sahakian disappeared through a door. It appeared they would not get a free peek at the back of the shop.

They walked around a minute, looking at the art and Remi wondering how much of it was legal. Every piece was good enough to be displayed in a top-tier museum. In fact, this gallery was like a museum in miniature. Cyril would love to see it.

Oh dear. Cyril. I haven't called him after our fight.

Well, he hasn't called me either.

But I should make the first move. I was being more unreasonable than he was.

Sahakian returned with a small woodcut slipped inside a sleeve of chemically inert clear plastic.

"Oh, I think he'd like this," Remi said. "It looks German. I'd say quite late in the 14th century. Perhaps even early 15th judging from the decoration on the border."

“Yes,” Sahakian agreed. “It’s a bit rare so I’m afraid I couldn’t part with it for less than $3,000.”

“That’s fine. If you could set that aside I think he’d be happy with it. He’d also prefer something a bit later, perhaps the 17th century. That’s his main focus.” Remi decided to stop beating around the bush or she’d be here all day. “I heard that a painting of one of the Four Horsemen of the Apocalypse by Jacob van der Veer has recently been put on the market.”

“I’ve heard of the artist, but I wasn’t aware he painted the Four Horsemen,” Sahakian said, glancing between Remi and Daniel and back again. “I haven’t seen anything by him on the market in a long time.”

Remi smiled, and leaned forward a little, speaking in a conspiratorial voice. “It’s just that our employer wants to get it before another person who we know is interested. He’s always had a rivalry with Montgomery Dyson.”

“But he’s dead!” Sahakian blurted, then froze, as if regretting his words.

Daniel cocked his head. “And how would you know that if it hasn’t been in the press?”

“I, um I mean … his attorney told me. We’ve done business in the past and he called this morning to inform me.”

Daniel shook his head. “We just talked with Mitchell, and he hasn’t told anyone.”

Daniel pulled out his FBI identification. “Azad Sahakian, I am placing you under arrest on suspicion of the murder of Montgomery Dyson.”

Remi took a step back, putting her hand in her purse and grasping her pepper spray.

But the art dealer didn’t resist. He stood there, silent and stony faced as a statue, as Daniel put the cuffs on him.

We’re done so soon?

Remi’s satisfaction was overwhelmed by regret. She’d be back to teaching undergraduates tomorrow.

CHAPTER NINE

As the FBI had warned them, Azad Sahakian had an excellent lawyer on retainer.

Remi sat with Daniel across from a bare table in an interrogation room while the art dealer and his attorney whispered in each other's ear. On the last case she had never been allowed to be present for an interrogation. This time she had insisted, explaining to Daniel that only she had the expertise to catch out Sahakian in a lie.

When they finally stopped whispering, it was the attorney, not the art dealer, who spoke.

"My client has no knowledge of the crime you are referring to," he told them.

Daniel's eyes narrowed. "So how did he know Dyson was dead?"

"Dyson's attorney, Frederick Mitchell, told him."

Remi and Daniel exchanged glances.

"Mitchell said he didn't tell anyone except the beneficiaries in Dyson's will," Daniel said.

The two went back to whispering. Remi began to grow impatient.

The lawyer turned back to them.

"Technically, my client is a beneficiary. He is on the board of the Harlem Art School, and Mr. Dyson left a substantial donation in his will."

This man is on the board of a charity? Remi thought, fuming. She struggled to focus on what the lawyer was saying. There were going to be lies in here somewhere, and she needed to spot them.

"So my client wasn't lying. Furthermore, Mr. Mitchell was concerned about the fact that Mr. Dyson was murdered apparently for a painting he had just purchased from my client. This was a painting of Death by the Flemish artist Jacob van der Veer. My client purchased this painting through regular channels with a certificate of legality and authenticity."

Remi couldn't believe what she was hearing. If her Belgian friend had been able to so quickly discover the painting was stolen, Sahakian should have been able to as well. Of course, the painting probably had come with a "certificate of legality and authenticity." Those looted Iraqi and Afghani treasures probably did too.

The only use those certificates had was as toilet tissue.

Remi supposed they were only admitting to the sale of the painting because there was some sort of paper trail that they figured the authorities would eventually uncover.

The lawyer went on.

"As soon as Mr. Mitchell heard the details of the break-in and murder, he phoned Mr. Sahakian to warn him and ask him about the painting and why that might be a motive in Mr. Dyson's killing."

The lawyer turned to the corrupt art dealer and raised an eyebrow. Sahakian gave a little nod, turned to Daniel and Remi, and took up the narrative.

"Mr. Dyson contacted me because I've developed a reputation for finding works of art that other dealers cannot."

I bet you have, thought Remi.

"He had heard through channels that Van der Veer's painting of Death was in the collection of an elderly heiress named Ursula Boone here in New York City who had recently died. I contacted the estate and convinced them to sell. All of that is aboveboard and I have certificates for everything."

Someone who is honest doesn't feel the urge to say that. Twice.

"Mr. Dyson was over the moon," Sahakian said. "He was so anxious to get a hold of this piece. He must have called me three or four times a day as the deal was being finalized and the paperwork put in order. Finally, I had it, and told him it was in my possession. He drove down that very day and came over personally."

"Alone?" Daniel asked.

"Yes. Alone."

"How did he pay?"

"In cash."

"Did you give him a receipt?"

"Of course."

Silence hung over them for a moment. If he really did give Dyson a receipt, where had it gone to?

Remi had a feeling Sahakian wouldn't give up that information so easily, assuming he even knew.

She decided to ask a question of her own. "What did he say about the painting? Why did he want that particular piece?"

The art dealer gave a little shrug. "I'm not sure. He acted strangely. Almost obsessed. When I unveiled it for him, he stared and stared. I warned him that such a minor artist wouldn't increase in value, but he dismissed that. Mr. Dyson said he wanted it for his personal collection and that it wasn't an investment. He asked me about the history of the painting and its provenance. There's really not much information on that. Jacob van der Veer was only one of dozens of artists whose names have come down to us who were active in the Low Countries at that time. Only a few pieces of his survive. A couple of landscapes, a portrait of the wife of the mayor of Haarlem, and a few religious paintings. He was reasonably successful in his lifetime but never achieved real fame. So there isn't much information on his life. No one has ever written a biography or even a PhD thesis on him."

"And what about the provenance of the painting?" Daniel asked.

"Ms. Boone, the previous owner, had it in her possession for many years. The heirs found the original receipt among her papers. All aboveboard."

That's the third time you've tried to convince us of that, Remi thought.

She hated people like Sahakian, parasites on the worlds of art and archaeology. Somewhere there was a family in Europe who should own that painting. In Iraq and Afghanistan, there lay archaeological sites pillaged of their treasures, the scientific knowledge those sites once contained destroyed for the sake of a quick profit that no doubt went into the hands of some local warlord or Islamist militia.

"So why was Dyson so obsessed with this painting?" Daniel asked.

Sahakian raised his hands. "I don't know. He had asked me about it a couple of years ago and I told him I didn't know anything about it. I even had to look up Van der Veer; the artist was so obscure. Then he called me about it again a few weeks ago, having heard that Ms. Boone had it. Apparently, he knew she had it and wasn't interested in selling, but now that she was dead, he thought her heirs might be more amenable to a sale. None of them are collectors. So he had me act as a go-between."

"Why you?" Remi asked. Dyson was a leading businessman. He didn't need some sketchy art dealer to do his business dealings for him.

"For my expertise in art and dealing with estate sales."

More like your expertise in faking certificates.

Remi gave Daniel a significant look.

The FBI agent told the suspect and his lawyer, "We'll be back in one minute."

They rose and left. Out in the hall, Daniel turned to her.

"What do you think?"

"I'm not sure what to think," Remi admitted, "except that he isn't telling us the whole truth."

"No, he is not."

"Have you ordered a search of his home and gallery?" Remi asked.

"Of course. We'll be going through his stock and his paperwork with a fine-toothed comb."

"Even if we don't find the painting, I bet we'll find some good evidence to bring him up on charges of dealing in stolen goods," Remi said.

Daniel smiled. "We?"

Remi gave a little shrug, chuckling. "I'm part of this investigation, aren't I?"

"You sure are, Agent Laurent." Even though Daniel meant that as a joke, Remi beamed with pride. "We'll let Sahakian stew for a while. The local police are sure to find something juicy at his place. In the meantime, why don't you research that painting. I want to know why one of America's richest men was obsessed by it, and why someone, maybe Sahakian or someone he knows, killed for it."

"I'll get to work," she replied breathlessly. This was turning out like the cryptex case, where an antique had inspired a desperate hunt, and a murder.

CHAPTER TEN

Paris, France
7:00 p.m.

In his long and lucrative career as an art dealer, Pierre Lafontaine had enjoyed many coups, many profitable sales and lucky purchases, but this latest acquisition beat them all.

An oil painting of War, one of the Four Horsemen of the Apocalypse, by Jan Mertens, a Flemish painter of the 17th century.

Lafontaine stood at a long worktable of scarred wood in the back room of his gallery, which he had closed early. He had just acquired the War painting, and he itched to study it.

So, standing at the worktable amidst various old frames, paintings wrapped for shipping, and some secondary artworks he didn't have room for in the front room, he studied the high point of his career.

It showed War as a fully armored figure, the visor of his helmet pulled up to reveal a skull instead of a face. He had his arm raised high, preparing to strike with a longsword at a crowd of pleading men and women. All wore wealthy clothing and symbolized the various elites of the day. In front, about to get cut down, was a fat burgher in an ermine cloak. Just behind him cowered his young trophy wife bedecked in jewels. A pot-bellied priest tried to flee, looking over his shoulder in horror at the grim fate sweeping into the scene.

Kneeling on the ground, the only person with his back turned to War, was a scholar. He hunched over a book as if in prayer.

But the book was no Bible or psalter. It was an astronomical text. Tiny stars could be seen on one page, almost too small to make out with Lafontaine's age-weakened eyes.

Lafontaine was seventy-five years old, and if his eyes weren't what they had once been, his mind was as sharp as ever. He knew the book was the key.

Pulling out a powerful magnifying glass and switching on a spot lamp, he bent over the painting, peering at the tiny page.

"Yes, yes. Of course," he murmured. "Why didn't I think of it before?"

Yes, the book was the key.

Or one part of the key. This was one of four paintings, all done by different Flemish artists. Four friends who had each painted one-fourth of the puzzle for the same wealthy client.

A puzzle he would solve.

Because he knew where at least one other painting was. He would leave in the morning to get it.

The sound of movement at the doorway to the front room did not make him look up.

"Your tea, sir," his assistant Guillaume said.

"Set it on the side table," Lafontaine said, still peering through his magnifying glass.

Tea? This calls for champagne!

Still studying, he heard Guillaume leave. Then there was a thud from the front room. Lafontaine shook his head. Guillaume was a sharp student, but a bit clumsy.

He heard footsteps at the door again.

"What did you bump into this time, Guillaume?" Lafontaine grumbled. "Nothing valuable, I hope."

"Step away from the painting."

This command came in English, a language Lafontaine did not speak well.

It took him a second to process it. Then, with a chill running through his body, he looked up.

A man stood in the doorway wearing a full suit of armor, a sword gripped in his left hand. He lifted his visor up to reveal a face twisted with rage.

"Step away from the painting," he said again.

Lafontaine did as he was told, raising his hands to calm the man.

"Guillaume!" he cried in a shaky voice.

The intruder gave him a smug smile and shook his head.

Lafontaine tried to remember his English.

"I … have money. In the, um, box. I give thousands."

The man clanked toward him.

"Wait! No! I give money."

The man in the suit of armor raised his sword up high.

Lafontaine turned and ran. There was no back door in this room, but there was a bathroom. Maybe if he barred himself inside, he could hold off this maniac until help came. Guillaume, if he was still alive, must be out on the street screaming for the police this very instant.

The clanking behind him grew in pace. While the maniac looked half his age, the armor slowed him down and terror sped Lafontaine up.

He got to the bathroom, slammed the door behind him, and put the ridiculously tiny metal hook through the eye on the doorframe to lock it.

Then he backed up to the far wall, only a couple of steps away. He reached for the mobile phone in his pocket to call the police, only to remember he had left it on his desk.

Lafontaine stared at the door, ears straining.

For a moment, silence.

Then the door cracked as the top half of the sword blade bit through the flimsy wood.

Lafontaine screamed. The madman wrenched the sword free, taking a large hunk of the door with it, then hacked at it again.

The door splintered, allowing enough room for the killer to bend over and step through.

Still screaming, Lafontaine picked up a ceramic soap dish and threw it with all his might.

It shattered on the metal helmet.

In the enclosed space of the bathroom, the killer didn't have room to swing his sword. Instead, he jabbed Lafontaine in the stomach.

The art dealer gasped as the cold steel sunk several inches into his middle.

The killer yanked it free. Lafontaine slumped against the sink, holding his gut, eyes half closed as he groaned in pain.

He didn't even see the next stab, which got him in the side.

Lafontaine's knees buckled, flashing with pain as they hit the tile floor. The killer stepped back as far as he could, reversed the sword, and jabbed down.

The blade bit into Lafontaine's neck.

His head spun. The pain began to recede as the room around him grew dim. Lafontaine fell flat on the floor, and his last vision in this life was of the killer stepping through the hole in the door and walking out of sight.

CHAPTER ELEVEN

Remi sat in front of her computer researching the painting by Jacob van der Veer. This was, she realized, not much different than a usual workday at Georgetown or the Sorbonne. When she wasn't burrowing into some dusty old archive, she was in front of a computer, researching old art or working on an academic paper.

The only difference now was that she was in a hotel room in New York City researching a painting that was stolen in a murder case.

And that made all the difference.

It had turned her research from a soothing intellectual stimulus into an exciting and far more important quest.

It was only a few hours after Daniel had arrested Azad Sahakian, and the art dealer was already out on bail. Daniel had explained to her that usually murder suspects weren't let out on bail, but since the evidence was thin, his lawyer had gotten the judge to reconsider. Now the New York Police Department was helping Daniel check on the validity of all of Sahakian's import licenses.

"If we can't make the murder rap stick," he had told her over the phone an hour ago, "I think we'll be able to get him on antiquities laws."

Good. People like that deserved to get punished by the law. But to do so, Remi had discovered, took a great deal of digging, legwork, and research. Daniel had been gone all afternoon looking at forms and making calls, while Remi had stayed in her cramped hotel room, which at least offered a fine view of downtown Manhattan.

Her research had uncovered some interesting facts that she was eager to tell Daniel whenever he got back from the police department. He'd probably have some good input.

As she had suspected, Death was only one of four paintings, each being a portrait of one of the Four Horsemen of the Apocalypse. Unusually, it was the only one painted by Jacob van der Veer. The others were all painted by his contemporaries. War was painted by Jan Mertens, Pestilence by Geert Janssens, and Famine by Frerik Peeters.

She had heard of none of these painters. While 17th century Flemish art was hardly her specialty, she was well-versed enough in all periods to know all the major figures. None of the four artists were major figures, and yet no less a personage than the mayor of Haarlem had hired them to make the set of paintings. During the 17th century, this city near Amsterdam was in its golden age, making vast fortunes off international trade and the production of linen and silk. The mayor had even hired Van der Veer to paint a portrait of his wife.

The mayor had been one of the richest men in the Low Countries at that time, owning several textile manufactories and a small fleet of ships. Why didn't he hire Rubens or Stevens or Brueghel the Younger? He could have afforded them.

Instead, he went with four capable but second-tier painters. Why? None of them were even from Haarlem. And why not just hire one man to paint all four?

Was it to add a little anonymity to the project? If Ruben took on a commission from a wealthy patron, the entire country would have heard about it. If someone like Mertens or Peeters took a commission of just a single midsized painting, it would make much less of a ripple.

But why want anonymity for a set of paintings, items whose purpose was to be displayed? And the paintings were signed.

It made no sense.

She needed to learn more. There was frustratingly little about any of these artists online, and a trip to the New York Public Library hadn't produced much else of value. Few paintings or biographical details existed for the four painters. What she did find was that at least a couple of them were known for their grim paintings of battles and apocalyptic scenes. Remi suspected all four of them had produced work along those lines, but there was simply not enough information to know for sure. Historians didn't even know the dates of birth or death for Mertens or Peeters.

She had, however, found photos of Pestilence and War in an old exhibition catalogue from 1925, when they appeared with other paintings of a religious bent in an exhibition in Amsterdam. Unfortunately, the photo was small and showed them hanging side by side, thus providing little detail. The caption, as much as she could puzzle out from the Dutch, said nothing beyond the names of the paintings and the artists.

Eleah Smets, her art curator friend in Brussels, had sent her a little more information. There was no record at all of the provenance of Famine by Frerik Peeters. That was unusual. No bill of sale, no museum catalog, no police report saying it was stolen. Perhaps it had been stolen or destroyed in a fire in an early century. While War and Pestilence did not appear to have been stolen or destroyed, there was no record of who owned them now. In the credits of the exhibition catalog, she discovered a list of the loaned items and was able to find family names for those who had loaned Pestilence and War. She sent these to Smets and was waiting for her answer.

Remi stared at the photo she had taken from the exhibition catalog. The four paintings had been commissioned together, but there was no record as to where they went after the painters completed them. Did the mayor of Haarlem keep them, or did he send the set to a colleague? Or did he disperse the paintings? As far as she could tell, the paintings had never all been owned by the same person, although the records were so incomplete that she couldn't say that for sure. That exhibition was the only time she could find where more than one had even been displayed together.

That made her wonder. What if the killer wanted all four? Often with sets of paintings, such as a religious triptych or paintings of the Apostles, there would be symbols scattered in each of the works, and the viewer could only understand them as a whole.

Was the man who stole Death looking for the other three?

If so, he would have a very difficult search. Remi could trace no record as to their present location.

And yet the murderer had found the painting of Death and had even known the very day Dyson purchased it.

This man was better informed than Remi, that was for sure.

Enough speculation. She went back to her research, chasing up leads as well as she could in online databases and digitized books.

A knock at her hotel room door stopped her. She went and peeked through the peephole, a precaution she had learned from Daniel. After what she had faced on the last case, she had come to appreciate the value of caution. Not as much as her new partner would like, she thought with a wry smile, but she was getting there.

Daniel stood in the hallway. She let him in.

"I just got off the phone with the FBI," he said breathlessly. Remi got the impression he ran here. "There's been a second murder."

Remi slowly sat down in her chair, stunned. She had predicted this. The murderer really was after all four paintings.

"Tell me more." Her voice came out harsh, barely above a whisper.

"The FBI is part of an international crime tracking system. I had the techies back at Quantico send me alerts if anyone related to the art world got killed or had a painting stolen. Last night in Paris an art dealer was hacked to death with a sword and his assistant bludgeoned with the pommel."

"I'm sorry, the what?"

"The knob on the end of the hilt, the handle of the sword."

"Oh, *le pommeau*. Go on."

"He was knocked out and is recovering in the hospital. They're still pumping him for information, but a search through the business receipts shows the murder victim just bought a painting of War by—" Daniel checked his phone for the name.

"By Jan Mertens," Remi said.

Daniel smiled and cocked his head. "Been doing some research, eh?"

"I have to do something while you're in the police station. As I suspected, the painting of Death was part of a set. Each was painted by a different Flemish artist for the same commission. This must be the same murderer!"

"Well, the M.O. is certainly the same."

"M.O.?"

"*Modus operandi* means the way someone operates. Criminals fall into patterns, even when they try to hide it, which this guy isn't. A ton of witnesses saw him go into the gallery, because he was dressed as a knight in full armor with a sword at his side."

"And no one called the police?"

"People thought he was in a movie, or it was some publicity stunt. The Paris police collected a ton of cell phone photos from people who saw him, but they all look like this."

Daniel showed her a photo. It showed a man walking down a narrow back street somewhere in central Paris. The visor to the helmet was down, so there was no telling the man's features. In fact, Remi only assumed he was a man because of the person's size.

"Dressed as a murderous monk last time, and this time as a knight," Daniel said.

"He's playing the part. Death with a scythe, and a knight of war."

"Yup. A psycho sickball, to use the technical term."

"We need to go to Paris," she said, moving to the edge of her seat.

Daniel shook his head. "It's a bit outside our jurisdiction. The FBI deals with crimes on U.S. soil."

"But this is a crime on U.S. soil. He killed an American citizen. Surely we could get clearance with Interpol to go—"

"There's that 'we' again. You're as eager as a rookie straight out of the academy."

"In a way I feel I am."

Daniel looked uncomfortable for a moment. "You're not. You are a huge help, but you have to remember you're a civilian advisor. You don't get a gun, and you don't get to chase suspects. You nearly got killed last time and if you get killed on this case, I'll have to live with that for the rest of my life."

Hot anger rose up in Remi's chest. He was dismissing her, putting her in a second category below him. She had been the one who had solved the Cryptex Killer case, and she would solve this one too, if she could convince this boor to go to Paris.

Guilt quickly tinged her anger. Taking it from Daniel's point of view, she could be seen as a liability. She really had put herself in harm's way several times on the last case, and if she had gotten hurt on Daniel's watch, it might cost him his job.

She needed to tread carefully to get what she wanted without alienating her partner.

"You're right," she said with some effort. "I need to be more careful. But we really need to chase up this case, Daniel. Both times when he stole the paintings he killed unnecessarily. Dyson was an old man. The killer could have overcome him easily. And in Paris he knocked out the assistant but killed the owner of the painting. He could have knocked out both, but he wanted to murder the man he was robbing."

"And no one else," Daniel mused. "He didn't bother killing the gallery assistant in Paris or any of the staff in East Hampton. Yes, I see what you mean. He's a focused killer, and he won't stop until he's killed the owners of all four paintings and taken them for himself."

"We need to convince your superiors to send us to Paris. If the killer is there, there's nothing further to investigate here."

She stared at the FBI agent as he said nothing, lost in thought.

At last Daniel nodded and got on his phone. Remi's heart lifted. He punched in a number, then stopped.

He looked Remi in the eye.

"One thing you might not know about killers. While some are selective, they get a whole lot less selective if you try and stop them. You need to be careful, Remi. This guy might be as dangerous as the Cryptex Killer."

Daniel got on his phone to talk with the FBI. Remi turned back to her computer to search for more information on the paintings and found the words going into the search engine coming out as gibberish.

Her hands couldn't stop shaking.

Then another trouble arose in her mind.

She still hadn't spoken with Cyril since their blowup at the Italian restaurant. If she was going to Paris, she needed to speak with him. She couldn't just run off to another country without informing him. After all, he was her department head as well as her lover.

But what to say?

Reluctantly, Remi pulled out her phone. Daniel stood not two meters away, talking with someone at the FBI. She couldn't make this call in his presence, and she couldn't very well make him leave. She'd have to explain why.

Gesturing to her phone, she headed out to the hallway. Daniel nodded, not really focusing, already deep in his struggle with government bureaucracy.

Stepping out into the hall and closing the door behind her, she checked her phone. No calls or texts from Cyril. She checked the time and saw he'd be done with classes and office hours.

Taking a deep breath, she dialed.

It rang and rang again. It rang a third time and Remi's tensions rose higher. Cyril always answered his phone on the first or second ring, even when in the middle of a conversation. He whipped it out of his pocket in his curt, businesslike manner and answered it like he was an executive negotiating the sale of ten-thousand shares.

Except this time, he didn't.

Was he in a meeting? She didn't know of any, and it wasn't his day to volunteer. Had Cyril seen who was calling and simply decided not to answer?

It rang again. And again.

She was about to hang up when he answered.

On the eighth ring.

"Yes," he demanded as if some phone salesman had interrupted his nap.

Already he was irritating her! Remi decided to keep her voice calm.

"It's me. I'm still in New York."

"The dean told me. Off on a big adventure."

"Sarcasm doesn't become you. We're making good progress on the investigation."

Cyril let out a loud, dramatic sigh. "I suppose it's necessary. Was your rudeness at the restaurant necessary?"

"I overreacted," Remi said, then bridled at this apology when it wasn't immediately followed by an apology of Cyril's own. After a brief pause, she continued. "But you should have been more understanding."

"Of what, exactly? You cutting off the most important conversation of our lives to talk about going off on some research trip? And then saying you have to chase some murderer? It feels like I don't know you anymore. You're changing, and not in a good way."

"And what's that supposed to mean?"

"All this policework. It excites you more than your research. And you're still after the cryptex, aren't you? That's why you want to go to Florence. There's some evidence there you want to dig up."

Remi grimaced. Cyril was too intelligent to hide the truth from.

"And what of it?" she said. "It's my main line of research, and it's been bolstered now that the cryptex has been shown to be real."

"But the Vatican took it, and you'll never see it again." He sounded smug about it, and that annoyed her to no end.

"So what? I can still research it. I took—" Remi stopped herself. She had almost revealed that she had opened it and took photos of the interior. "—I found some new evidence for a groundbreaking paper. But that's not what I want to talk about. There's been a development in the case."

"Oh God, more policework. I thought you were only going to New York for a day to study a crime scene."

"I never said that," Remi glared at the phone. He was so eager to keep her on a leash, he heard what he wanted to hear.

"Yes, you did. And you're going to stay in New York for days now, aren't you? While Edwards and Hinksey have to scramble their schedules to cover your classes. The dean has prostrated himself to the FBI."

Remi gathered her patience, took a deep breath, and said, "I'm not staying in New York. Actually, the case is taking us to Paris."

"What?!"

"Don't get hysterical. The killer is looking for a series of paintings, and it appears he isn't done killing."

"Oh God, you're looking for another serial killer. How can you do this to me?"

Remi's brow furrowed. "Do this to you?"

"Leave me like this! You embarrassed me in the restaurant, and now you're leaving me alone to go off one some ridiculous quest for a killer in Europe."

"It's not some ridiculous quest. It's valuable policework."

"Leave it to the police then."

"I am the police," she blurted.

Right after she said it, she realized how ridiculous it sounded.

So did Cyril. He laughed. Actually *laughed.*

"Oh, Remi. I never suspected this side of you," he said, still laughing. "You're like a little girl with her head full of adventure. Get real. You're an academic and you're about to get—"

"Enough!" she snapped. "I'm my own person and I'll do what I like in my life. You have no right to be so condescending and possessive. I can see why your wife left you!"

With that, she hung up.

Remi slumped against the wall, feeling sick. What just happened? Had he really been so terrible, and had she really been so cruel?

Just as a new case was beginning, she could feel her relationship falling apart.

CHAPTER TWELVE

One whole day, Remi fumed as she sat in a cramped economy seat on a 747 flying across the Atlantic.

They had wasted an entire day getting approval through the grinding bureaucracy of the FBI and Interpol. By this time, the killer could be anywhere. He might have even killed again.

How can these bureaucratic fools hold up a murder investigation for a full day while they fill out forms? No wonder so many international criminals got away with their crimes.

And the wasted day had allowed the media to catch up. The story of a murder of an art dealer by a man in full armor went viral, with numerous photos of him circulating on the Internet. The French media was abuzz with speculation, and the international media had picked it up too.

Dyson's business enterprises had been obliged to announce his death, citing "as yet unknown causes." The press release cited his age and his previous battle with cancer as a way to deflect any suspicion of foul play. Of course, sooner or later that would come out too.

Remi and Daniel didn't need the media involved. It would only complicate things. If the FBI had granted their travel request immediately, they might have already solved the case and the media attention wouldn't matter.

At least the extra day had given Cyril plenty of time to sulk. She had texted him saying that the case would take longer than she had expected. He didn't reply. Then, when the flight to Paris cleared, she texted him again to tell him they were going to France. She explained how necessary it was. She even apologized for having to leave the country.

She did not, however, apologize for the things she had said. She would, but only after he had apologized first.

Again, he didn't reply.

A distinguished historian and scholar, sulking like a schoolboy who didn't get what he wanted for Christmas!

She decided she wouldn't send any more texts. It was his turn to reach out.

Remi stared out the window at the bright blank canvas of the North Atlantic. While the weather was clear, they were too high up to see any boats. She could see nothing but blue sky and green, glittering water.

"Excited about seeing home?" Daniel asked.

"Pardon?" Remi asked, coming out of her reverie.

"I asked if you were excited about seeing home."

"Certainly. I haven't been back for more than three months. I'm not sure I'll have much time to see family, though."

Daniel turned away and looked gloomily at the back of the seat in front of him. "On this job you don't have much time to see family even if you're living with them."

Remi remembered his quip about being divorced and realized he had been telling the truth.

Not quite sure what to say, she decided to stay on safe ground. "Actually, my mother lives on the family farm. Quite some distance from Paris. A cousin and his wife live there too."

"Hmm, that's too bad. I don't think we'll have time for a road trip."

"You'd like it. The farm is beautiful. Fine local produce too."

"I bet. We'll have to get some good dining in on the FBI's tab," Daniel said, patting his stomach. "Revenge for putting us in coach."

"I wasn't expecting them to fly us first class."

"You're learning."

They both laughed. This man had a talent for making her feel better, even when he didn't know she was down.

"So have you visited Paris before?" Remi asked. He had mentioned a few trips to Europe when he was younger.

Daniel's face darkened.

"Yeah, I've been there," he grumbled, not looking at her.

Remi stared at him for a moment before looking away.

What's this moodiness? I've seen it before, and it's always related to Europe or fine art. I don't understand why those things would bother him.

She decided to change the subject.

"I can look through the Paris archives. Much of that material isn't online. I might find some more information about the paintings."

"Good," he said with a curt nod.

The past day of investigation hadn't turned up much. Remi had discovered no important information about the four paintings or their painters, and no new material evidence in the crimes had come up. Now that there had been another murder, the seedy art dealer was off the hook, although the FBI was still rifling through his records for evidence of trafficking in stolen art and antiquities.

"I wonder if he's an American going to France or a Frenchman going home?" Remi said.

"Good question. The gallery assistant never heard the man speak. He simply clanked into the gallery, the assistant made some joke, and then got conked over the head."

"Bizarre."

"Makes you wonder what he'll do for famine and pestilence."

Remi made a face. "Let's catch him before he gets the chance to show us."

Daniel looked at her again. "Thanks for taking the time out to do this. Your expertise is a real help, and your French will be an even bigger help."

"That's all right. I enjoy it."

"Yeah, I noticed. So everything cleared away with your department?"

"Your supervisor called the dean and explained the situation. It's all taken care of. Georgetown has good Criminal Studies and Criminal Law departments. They want to maintain positive relations with law enforcement. I believe Assistant Director Ochiai promised to send some guest speakers."

Daniel groaned. "Oh God, I hope she didn't volunteer me. I got enough to do."

"That's right, you mentioned you don't like academia."

"No."

His tone warned her off pursuing that track. Before she could think of something to say, he asked,

"So how's your fiancée? I hope he's not upset about you flying to the City of Love without him."

"Oh, no! He's very supportive of everything I do."

Why did I just say that?

Because you barely know this man and you're too embarrassed to tell the truth, that's why.

"That's great," Daniel said.

"Yes, he's the best. An academic like me."

"Yeah, he's your department head."

Remi didn't recall telling him that, but of course he would have done a background check on her.

That felt a bit invasive. While she didn't have anything to hide, she didn't like this man knowing more, perhaps far more, about her than she did about him.

If you want to work for the FBI, you have to expect them to check up on you.

That's something to consider. Do you really want this?

She didn't have an answer to that. Not yet.

"Sorry," Daniel said. Remi realized she had left a pause in the conversation. "I need to read up on the people we hire."

"It's understandable," she replied, still not feeling terribly comfortable.

"Don't worry, we didn't dig up any dirt. You don't really have any dirt. You need to change that boring life of yours." Daniel laughed.

I was just thinking the same thing.

"I've always been a bit bookish," Remi admitted.

Daniel nudged her. "When you weren't blasting away at targets with your dad."

"True."

"Well, if you need a letter of recommendation for your fiancée, I'd be happy to write one. I'll tell him you've been a good scholar and a good shot. You guys set a date yet?"

"Um, no," Remi said, shifting in her uncomfortable seat. "Busy careers. We'll probably wait until later in the year."

"Oh, that's perfect. If you marry an American, you can get a green card. That would make it much easier to hire you as a consultant. You could even get a gun license. Not sure if the FBI would let you carry on a case, though. Looks like you have everything all set up."

"Oh yes, it's all working out."

Remi put on a brave smile. Inside, though, her emotions were in turmoil. Pretending everything was all right with Cyril made her feel terrible, made every clash with him feel twice as bad as it had been.

Daniel did have a point, though. If she married Cyril, she wouldn't have to worry about her expiring work visa. She wouldn't have to worry about having an unclear status with the FBI either.

She'd only have to worry about being married to Cyril.

Assuming that even happened. After their mutual blowup, Cyril might be having second thoughts.

No time to sort that out now. She had a case to work on.

While they had not found sufficient records for the paintings in the United States, the archives in Europe might hold the answer. The killer had obviously accessed them, because he seemed to know far more about the paintings and their locations than they did.

Just like with the Cryptex Killer, they were playing a deadly game of Catch Me If You Can.

She needed to delve into the history of these paintings, and the obscure painters who made them, as well as the rich and who commissioned them. She needed to pore over the same records the killer had and pick out the same details he did.

Only then could she understood how this bizarre man thought, and what he would do next.

CHAPTER THIRTEEN

This was not how Remi expected to return to Paris. She had imagined a little crowd of friends and colleagues giving her a party after a productive year at Georgetown and a triumphant return to the Sorbonne. Instead, she had told no one, and was red-eyed and sleepless after an overnight flight that got them into Paris early in the morning.

She was not headed to the Sorbonne, and she was not headed to an apartment of her own. Remi had ended her lease and put her things in storage before she had set off for the United States, and thus had no home in Paris to go to. Instead, she was headed to a cheap hotel in the company of an FBI agent. It all made her feel like a foreign visitor to her own country.

Sleepy, she stared blankly out the window of the taxi taking them from the airport, the familiar landmarks seeming distant and strange. The ornate buildings, wide boulevards, and familiar shops should have felt like a homecoming, but she was not here to see friends and family. Somewhere in this city lurked a murderer.

Assuming he hadn't left for some other country. They still didn't know where the other two paintings were.

Daniel looked with interest as the taxi drove into central Paris and past the Eiffel Tower. He seemed far more accustomed to long flights.

Remi checked her phone and sat bolt upright. A missed call from Cyril, made in late evening, D.C. time, while Remi had still been in the air. He did not leave a voice message or text.

Finally, he was coming out of his sulk.

On instinct she started to dial, then stopped herself. Not now, not with Daniel sitting beside her. Besides, it was too late in the United States. Cyril would be fast asleep. Waking him up would be a bad start to the conversation. Better to have this talk when they were both rested.

They reached the hotel and Remi noted that while the FBI had done well on location, getting them a hotel in the city center, as usual they had skimped on price. It was a two-star place with a grim little lobby, small rooms, and no view. They went to their separate rooms and Remi unpacked and had a quick shower. Long flights with that recirculated air and Styrofoam food always made her feel dirty.

Her mind felt slow and confused. Jetlag threatened to pull her down to sleep. The narrow bed with second-rate linen beckoned.

No, she needed to focus on the case. She had fallen behind enough already. She would also have to call Cyril this evening once it was daytime on the American east coast.

She put Cyril from her mind. The quicker she got through this case, the quicker she could sort things out with him.

She left the hotel room and knocked on Daniel's door. He opened up, talking on the phone, and motioned for her to come in.

Even though he had been there only half an hour, Daniel's hotel room had turned into a disaster zone. His shoes lay on their side in the middle of the floor, a couple of shirts were draped over a chair, and the other contents of his suitcase spread over the bed, the desk, and the bathroom. As Daniel continued to talk on the phone, Remi looked about in wonder. How could a man so meticulous in his work be so slovenly in his personal life?

Daniel got off the phone. "That was Interpol. They're sending a man over in half an hour. He'll be working with us the whole way. After that, we'll head to the crime scene."

"We should go there now."

Daniel shook his head. "The local police don't want us there until Interpol shows."

Remi grunted. French bureaucracy and xenophobia. They trusted a local representative from Interpol far more than a visit from the FBI. As far as French officialdom was concerned, anybody was better than the Americans.

"At least that gives us time to get a coffee," Remi said.

"Excellent idea. Wouldn't want to yawn in this guy's face. Bad for international relations. I saw a Starbucks not far from here as we came in."

Remi clicked her tongue. "Barbarian. You're in one of the greatest cultural centers of the world and you want to go to an American chain? Come. I'll take you to a proper café."

Daniel gave a mock salute. "Yes, ma'am. What's the word for barbarian in French?"

"Barbare."

"Barbare," Daniel said in a deliberately bad French accent. "*Je suis barbare.* I am an uncouth American *barbare*, come here to save you from ze Germans a third time."

"Careful," Remi warned as they left the room.

"*Mon Dieu!* She will kill ze American *barbare* with ze *guillotine*!"

"You need some sleep."

"No time. Let's get some of ze *café au lait*."

"Oh, and we don't use the guillotine anymore. It was banned in 1981."

"Such a civilized nation."

"Says the representative of the country with the highest incarceration and execution rate in the developed world."

"*Touché, mon ami.* Yeah, the States is a mess."

"I've never understood why. You have so many resources. So much wealth and industry and great universities. It really is the land of opportunity."

Daniel shrugged. "I think that's what makes it worse. People think there's a shortcut to wealth, so they deal or steal. Others feel like if they aren't making it, they're total failures, and start taking drugs. That doesn't explain it all, though. You know, I was kind of sheltered in the Behavioral Affairs Unit. Serial killers are sick. You get them in every culture. It's easy to explain away the actions of someone who's mentally ill. But the regular cops I talk to …" Daniel shook his head and continued in a bitter tone. "They dealing with regular people every day, people who don't have mental problems. And they see more and more despair and violence among those people every year. We're slipping. We're really slipping."

The mock French accent had disappeared, as had the rest of the joking around. Remi could see that Daniel was seriously concerned about the fate of his nation. Among Europeans, cheering the decline of the United States was a favorite topic of conversation. She had done it herself. That boorish, arrogant people who tried to dictate to other countries how to run their affairs. And that nation's representatives in Paris—the hordes of potbellied, crass tourists—had not helped Remi's impression.

But now that she had spent a few months in the United States, and was in a deep relationship with an American, she had begun to see things in a different light. Yes, there was boorishness and insularity—Remi couldn't count the number of times she had to explain where

France was—but there was also a great deal of good. Neighbors were generally friendly and did not put on airs like in France. And she had seen so much giving, so much volunteerism. Like Cyril, a leading intellectual who gave his time to teach high school dropouts how to read.

Cyril. She needed to call Cyril.

Later. He was asleep. It was a relief that she couldn't call him now, she'd prefer to put it off, but by putting it off it remained hanging over her head like the sword of Damocles.

Tonight. I'll call him tonight after we've put in a good day's work, and I get some rest.

The café made her feel better. It was a little place with a glass front and an open door out of which wafted the smells of freshly brewed coffee and freshly baked bread. They sat outside at a little wrought iron table, watching the passersby. All around her she heard French in that beautiful Parisian dialect, the highest form of her language ever developed.

Just like home, she thought.

Wait, I am home.

Or is home Georgetown University?

"I'll order for you," she told Daniel to get her mind off that awkward topic. "What would you like?"

"The strongest coffee they have and a croissant."

"A croissant?" Remi asked with a smile. "You're becoming French already."

"Actually the croissant was invented in Vienna after they pushed back the Turks in 1683. The local bakers made their pastries into the crescent shape after the crescent moon on the Ottoman flag. Sort of one-upping the enemy by eating him."

"You and your historical facts. It doesn't matter who invented it. We perfected it."

Daniel only smiled and called the man from Interpol to tell him their new location.

She summoned a waiter, who ignored her for a good five minutes until he actually came. Remi had forgotten that European waiters made salaries and didn't rely on tips like American waiters. It made them much more relaxed about their duties.

That gave Daniel a chance to bring up the police report the Paris gendarmerie had sent. It was in French, a casual snub to Daniel, so Remi started reading it.

The waiter was forgiven when he brought the coffee and croissants, brewed and baked to perfection. The partners descended into silence as they enjoyed their breakfast. Remi's fatigue and tension eased. It was enjoyable sitting with this interesting, multifaceted American, so unlike the academics she usually socialized with.

It was also interesting to read a police report. It reminded her of her father, who had written so many. That made her feel a bit sad. That poor man had been so dedicated to his job that he had worked himself into an early grave. He had really cared about making the streets safe. So did Daniel. He worked too much too.

Says the woman reading a murder report on jetlag.

She kept reading, hoping to find a clue. There had to be something to help in the mass of facts and photos.

They were on their second much-needed coffee, and Daniel was on his third chocolate croissant, when a tall, thin Scandinavian man walked up to their table. He looked in his early forties with angular features and a shock of blonde hair.

Remi sat upright, studying him, all senses alert.

"Agents Walker and Laurent?" he asked in French.

"I'm Daniel Walker," her partner said, understanding the question enough to answer.

"And I'm Professor Remi Laurent. I'm not an agent," she replied in French, feeling a bit embarrassed to admit this. "I'm a civilian consultant."

"Ah yes, my mistake. Pleased to make your acquaintance, Professor Laurent. I'm agent Nels Torsson, your liaison with Interpol."

He said this in the correct, careful, and somewhat slow diction of a man approaching fluency. Remi relaxed. For a moment she had had visions of getting attacked by the killer they were hunting.

"Your French is quite good, Agent Torsson. Have you lived in France long?" she asked.

"Only a year. I'm Swedish but my grandmother was French. I sued to spend summers on her farm in Bordeaux."

"Oh, really? My grandmother had a farm in Provence. I loved those days."

Daniel cut in. "Um, could we speak in English, maybe?"

"Oh, I'm terribly sorry," Agent Torsson said, his pale face going red as he switched to near-perfect English. "I thought you spoke French since you were on this assignment."

"No, I'm on this assignment because of my charming nature and predilection for beating suspects."

Torsson looked like he wasn't sure if that was a joke or not. Remi wasn't sure either.

"Sit down, Agent Torsson," Daniel said. "And let's plan strategy. Want a chocolate croissant? They're awesome. Not as good as Dunkin' Donuts, but when in Rome, eh? Well, Paris. Whatever."

Torsson gave Remi's partner an unreadable look and sat down.

"I've spoken with my superiors at Interpol, and we have their full support," Torsson said. "They understand the gravity of this crime and that there will, in all likelihood, be two more. Have you tracked down the ownership of the other two paintings?"

"Not yet," Daniel said. "Remi here was hoping to find some more information in the Paris archives."

"And I think I better get to work," she said. "What will you gentlemen be doing this afternoon?"

Torsson and Daniel exchanged glances.

"I can show you the crime scene and what the investigators have discovered," the Swede offered.

"Sounds good. Remi, give me a call if you're done by lunch time. If your restaurant recommendations are as good as your café tips, I'm sticking with you for every meal."

* * *

It turned out Remi did not meet Daniel and Torsson for lunch. She found far too much of value sitting in a little cubicle in the Louvre archives. It was a part of the famous museum few people ever saw, an annex filled with books, exhibition catalogs, and the personal papers of thousands of people associated with the art world. It took a few hours of digging, and another coffee to stave off creeping jetlag, but she finally struck gold.

It was in the catalog of an auction house that had sold a couple of minor 17th century Flemish works from the Louvre's collection forty years ago. It wasn't uncommon for museums to sell parts of their collection in order to raise funds, although they generally limited it to works of secondary importance that weren't vital to the nation's culture. The Louvre would never sell the Mona Lisa, for example.

The paintings the Louvre sold at that auction did not interest her; it was what else had been sold that was vital—Pestilence by Geert Janssens.

Remi sat for a moment, stunned.

The image was a full page in color and showed the painting in perfect detail.

Pestilence rode a black horse and was depicted as a gaunt man with pustules all over his face, arms, and hia bare, sunken chest. Unlike the other paintings, only the front half of the horse and its rider could be seen. The rest of the frame was taken up by a large crowd falling down to the ground and dying of the same horrible disease that Pestilence carried with him.

The scene was outside a tavern, a popular theme for paintings of the day. Usually they showed merry peasants drinking, dancing, and flirting. This painting was a mockery of the genre. Beautiful young women lay on the green lawn, their faces ravaged by disease. Red-nosed drinkers slumped over tables, their steins knocked over and the beer spattering to the ground. One man, near the door to the tavern, cried out in pain, raising one suppurating hand to point to the tavern's sign, a wooden board that showed a set of yellow stars on a blue background.

Remi stared. In another of the paintings, Death by Jacob van der Veer, the figure rode through a night sky that emphasized the pattern of the stars.

She pulled out the old photo of War and Pestilence hanging side by side in an exhibition from a century ago and looked more closely at the painting of War by Jan Mertens. That painting appeared to be set in the daytime, although the photo was of such poor quality it was hard to tell. One odd detail was that everyone was looking at War except for a man dressed as a scholar, who had his back to War and looked at a book.

Remi squinted, pulled out a magnifying glass and squinted again. Were those stars on the page of the scholar's book, or simply the graininess of the old photo?

She needed to follow up on that. Two paintings emphasized stars. If a third did, then most certainly the fourth did since they were commissioned by the same patron and painted by four colleagues. The stars might be significant.

But first, she needed to follow up this sale and find out who ended up with the painting of Pestilence.

Because that would be the killer's next victim.

CHAPTER FOURTEEN

As soon as Remi discovered the sales catalog including Pestilence by Geert Janssens, she called Daniel.

"Is that Interpol agent with you?"

"Torsson? Yeah, he's here."

"I discovered Pestilence was sold forty years ago. We need to track down who has it now and we need his legal authority to do that. If I make the call, they'll ignore me."

That's why I need to be officially with the FBI. They're going to have to listen to me if they want my help next time.

"I'll put him on," Daniel said.

She heard the phone being passed to the Interpol agent. Before he could even say hello, Remi poured out all the information she had learned. Sensing her urgency, all Torsson said was, "I'll get on it," and handed the phone back to Daniel.

"Good job, Remi. I knew I was right in getting you on board," the FBI agent said.

Remi smiled. "I hope Torsson can trace that painting to its present owner. Whoever it is will be on the killer's hit list."

"Our Swedish friend looks pretty competent to me. You eaten yet?" Daniel asked.

"No. Now that you mention it, I'm hungry. Have you eaten?"

"Yeah, we went to McDonald's an hour ago."

Remi stared at the phone. "McDonald's."

"Yeah."

"You're in one of the culinary capitols of the world and you went to McDonald's."

"They don't have Wendy's here."

Remi rubbed her temples. This man was going to be the death of her.

"I'm going to go get some food," she said. "Actual food."

"Righto. When I did a search for McDonald's I noticed one right next to the Louvre. You can get there in five minutes."

"Goodbye, Daniel."

She hung up.

* * *

Daniel shrugged. Remi seemed to be in a bad mood for some reason. Perhaps it was the jetlag.

As Torsson got on the phone to track down the lead, Daniel looked around the back room of Pierre Lafontaine's art gallery once again, not at the sad bloody scene in the bathroom down the hall, but here where the confrontation no doubt had taken place.

The worktable was strewn with tools, bits of canvas, and a few wrapped paintings. Lafontaine had been a bit messy. Only the end of the table was kept clear. Just enough room for a mid-sized painting like the one missing from Dyson's mansion. A spot lamp focused a soft light on the spot.

So Lafontaine had been standing here studying the painting when the murderer had clanked in and chased him into the bathroom.

Looked pretty straightforward, except for the motive. Nothing else appeared to have been stolen. He saw no missing spaces on the walls, and the bookshelf on the far wall was crammed to overflowing with volumes.

Daniel walked to the front room. The shutters in front had been brought down and a lone light shone, dimly illuminating the numerous Impressionist paintings adorning the walls. A female police officer stood there. Through an open doorway to the side, he could hear a faint sobbing.

"Is that assistant ready to talk?" he asked.

"Yes," the officer said in passable English. "And she speaks your language."

That came out almost as an accusation. Daniel shrugged. He didn't have time for any European attitude. Guillaume Blanchet, the assistant working in the front room, was still in the hospital. He had made his statement to the police and had nothing really to say other than a man in armor had walked into the gallery and conked him over the head.

Blanchet was suffering from a bad concussion and couldn't be questioned at length, but fortunately there had been another assistant on the scene, a woman named Béatrice Lavigne who had been upstairs in a workshop that was used for restoring artworks. The room was accessed from the back room through a door that happened to be hidden from view by a large canvas standing in the middle of the room showing a Napoleonic battle scene. The killer had apparently not realized the door to the upstairs was there, which was probably why Lavigne hadn't been assaulted like her boss and coworker.

Now it was time to question her.

He stepped through the doorway with the female officer and into a small viewing room. A few plush chairs in imitation Louis XIV style were arrayed in front of a blank wall with a strip of lighting above. Here paintings could be hung and put on various strengths and angles of lighting so potential buyers could inspect the work better.

Béatrice Lavigne sat on one of the chairs, wiping at her eyes and snuffling. She looked up when they came in, eyes going wide.

Fear? Guilt? Daniel wasn't sure. A lot of people acted nervous around the police, especially at a crime scene. That didn't mean they were guilty of anything.

"Do you speak English?" he asked.

"Y-yes."

"Tell me what happened, right from the beginning."

"I'm afraid there isn't much to tell," the young woman said in good English with traces of a posh English accent. Daniel figured she had studied for a time in London or Oxford. "I was upstairs restoring the gilt on an eighteenth-century frame. I heard some screaming downstairs and rushed down, thinking we were being robbed. I rushed down to the bottom of the stairs and suddenly got frightened, so I stopped."

"Then what happened?" Daniel asked gently as she wiped her eyes, trembling too much to continue. His first instinct was that she wasn't the killer and wasn't involved, but he suspended judgement until he heard more.

"I listened at the door for a moment and didn't hear anything except a strange metal clanking. I now know it was that insane man in armor. At the time I didn't know, and I listened until the clanking faded away. Then I plucked up the courage to open the door."

Béatrice Lavigne shuddered, wiped her eyes, and pulled herself together enough to continue.

"At first I didn't see anything amiss. Then I noticed Monsieur Lafontaine's painting was gone."

"What painting was that?" Daniel asked, deciding to play dumb. It was best when interrogating people to let them supply as much of the information as possible. They could reveal a lot that way.

"A Flemish painting from the 17th century. War by Jan Mertens. He had recently acquired it and was obsessed with its study. He gave up all other work. Guillaume and I had to work extra hours." Suddenly her eyes widened in realization. "Did the intruder steal it?"

"Yes," Daniel admitted. "Why did you assume that?"

Lavigne wiped her brow. "Monsieur Lafontaine acted very protective of it. He gave us strict instructions not to tell anyone he had purchased it, and not to let anyone in the back room where it might be seen. He also wanted to find the other three in the set, but he didn't want us researching it. That was odd, since he does most of his research while he oversees the buying and selling and any major restorations. He was so secretive about these paintings, which was unusual for him. We didn't understand what all the fuss was about. It isn't all that valuable."

"It's valuable to whoever came in here."

The gallery assistant nodded sadly. "When I noticed the painting was gone from its spot, I entered the room further and I saw the broken door to the bathroom. I went there and I … I … "

Béatrice Lavigne put her face in her hands and wept. Daniel, pitying her, rested a hand on her shoulder.

"Sorry to make you go through all that. Did your boss ever mention an American collector named Montgomery Dyson?"

After a moment to pull herself together, she replied, "No. But he worked with many people over the years."

"Never mind that for now. It appears the Four Horsemen of the Apocalypse were all painted by different artists?"

The young woman nodded.

"Did Monsieur Lafontaine have a database or library on these painters?"

Lavigne gestured to the back room. "The bookshelf has several volumes, and his computer has many documents. There is no one book on any of the painters. They were all minor. But he has pieced together information over the years from a number of sources."

"Do you have the password to his computer?"

"Yes."

"Hold on. That gives me an idea."

Daniel got back on the phone and called Remi.

"Hey Remi, where are you now?"

"Going to lunch at a proper restaurant." *Why did she stress those last two words?* "I've found all I can find at the Louvre."

"Eat quick and get over here," Daniel said. "We might just have found a gold mine of info."

"I'll order something to go."

"You can order to go in France?"

"You can if you're hunting a murderer."

She hung up. Daniel chuckled, knowing she'd be here as fast as the Parisian taxis could carry her.

And she'd come up with some good information too.

They needed it. It looked like their killer was still on the hunt.

CHAPTER FIFTEEN

Daniel had been right, there was a gold mine in Pierre Lafontaine's library and computer.

Well, at least a silver mine.

Remi and Béatrice pored over the research Monsieur Lafontaine had conducted on the paintings of the Four Horsemen of the Apocalypse and their painters—Death by Jacob van der Veer, War by Jan Mertens, Pestilence by Geert Janssens, and Famine by Frerik Peeters.

Lafontaine had been busy. He had assembled scraps of information from a dozen archives in France, the Netherlands, Belgium, and Germany. The man had hired a translator for the German archive material but knew Dutch himself. Remi wondered if he had taught himself the language in order to better research the four painters. This research certainly showed an obsession stretching back at least ten years. Remi didn't read the language, which left a gap in what she could read of Lafontaine's discoveries.

But she could see enough.

What was immediately apparent was that this was no simple art theft. Two different paintings in two different countries had been stolen, neither of major value. The owners did not appear to know one another. Béatrice had checked the customer database and found no record of the gallery ever having any contact with Montgomery Dyson.

Then there was the style of the thefts, imitating the subjects of the paintings themselves. Whoever was committing these killings had some other motive than just acquiring them. He wanted to make a point.

But what?

The answer must lie in the lives of the painters themselves, and their patron, the mayor of Haarlem.

And that's where it got interesting.

Remi had gotten a wrong impression about these artists through the surviving paintings of Jacob van der Veer. Of the few pieces of his to make it to the modern day, they were all relatively tame—two landscapes, some religious paintings of the apocalypse that were bloody but no bloodier than similar works of their type, and a portrait of the wife of the mayor of Haarlem.

Surviving paintings from the other members of the quartet told a different story.

Jan Mertens had not only painted the horseman of War; he had painted several paintings of battles and massacres in grisly detail. There was even a record of a patron refusing to pay for a commission because it was "of suche a bloode thirstie natur that mine familie shunned its verie presence." The patron asked for the painting to be toned down and Mertens had refused, stating that, "I painte the truthe, not the honied dreames of a burgher's fancie."

Mertens never got his money.

The other two were even worse. Geert Janssens was kicked out of Amsterdam for "unholy paintings." The records gave no details other than the fact that the paintings had been seized by church authorities and destroyed, and Geert Janssens was named *persona non grata* in Holland's greatest city.

Frerik Peeters did time in jail for the murder of a child before being released for "lack of evidence." While the details of the trial had been lost sometime over the ensuing centuries, this piqued Remi's curiosity. If there had been insufficient evidence to keep him in jail, how had the court found sufficient evidence to put him in there in the first place? Frerik Peeters was also known for contributing some rather macabre engravings to alchemical texts. While such texts were in great demand at the time, the examples she saw went far beyond what the Church accepted and that made him a figure of controversy. Many showed demons in a neutral or even positive light, quite unacceptable at the time. There were oblique references to Geert Janssens and Jacob Van der Veer also contributing to illustrations to books of alchemy, although none seem to have survived.

With three out of four of the artists having been involved in alchemy, Remi had to wonder if Jan Mertens had participated as well. Unfortunately, there was no evidence of this.

Sadly, despite Lafontaine's extensive research over the years, so little information had survived about these four minor artists that there were huge gaps in his data.

Still, the strangeness of the works, the common link of alchemy, and the similarity in style and tone between the four artists, hinted at some sort of collaboration before they had been commissioned by the mayor to paint the Four Horsemen.

Pierre Lafontaine had done some research on the mayor as well, but there he, and Remi, hit a dead end. Hendrick van Berckenrode held the post from 1622 to 1630, during the height of the city's wealth, but seemed to be nothing but a respectable, wealthy businessman who had come into a position of political power. He donated to the poor. He paid for repairs and an expansion to his local church. In his younger years he had been captain of the city militia. Not a whiff of scandal touched him. He had his political opponents, to be sure, but even they did not level any charges of corruption or impiety at his feet.

So why hire a religious dissident, an accused child murderer, and painters who dabbled in the controversial subject of alchemy? A man of his position would be scrutinized. Granted, he had chosen Jacob van der Veer, the least controversial of the four, to paint his wife, but even van der Veer had done illustrations for alchemical texts, something the more religious members of the Haarlem community would have looked at askance.

No, a man in such a position would not have risked political backlash over the artists he hired unless he absolutely needed to hire these particular men.

That hinted at some greater purpose. Remi knew that despite all the public displays of piety, many people in that era were fascinated by the darker side of life. Paintings of martyrdoms and military atrocities were popular. Public executions and freak shows drew large crowds. Some historians theorized that witch hunts actually uncovered a resurgent folk religion with a faith based on magic and nature worship outside the control of thc Church. Mysticism and alchemy, while claiming to be aligned with Christian teachings, often went far beyond mainstream doctrine and got their practitioners in trouble. Court documents from several nations recorded the discovery of numerous secret societies devoted to strange religious practices.

Perhaps Hendrick van Berckenrode and the four artists were members of one such society, a society that devoted itself to the macabre. It would explain the outré subject matter of so many of the paintings and well as the criminal records of two of the painters.

If so, Lafontaine had found no evidence of it beyond the works themselves. He also hadn't found any evidence of where the other paintings ended up. Of course, he didn't have police powers to demand that art dealers give up their sales records. Hopefully Torsson would be able to do better.

Because if not, this investigation would be stalled until the murderer showed himself for a third time.

* * *

While Remi busied herself with researching the artists, Daniel and Torsson were at the local precinct going through flight and police records.

Torsson had phoned a judge to try and fast-track a search warrant for sales files on the painting of Pestilence. While waiting for that to come back, they looked through flight records of people who had flown between the United States and France in between the times of the two murders and who also had criminal records in either the United States or the European Union.

The matching up took some time. There were dozens of flights a day between the two countries, flying from several different cities. A smart criminal would not have flown out of New York, the scene of the first murder. Instead, he would have tried to cover his tracks by flying out of a different city or even a different state. Daniel decided not to widen the search to Canada and Mexico yet. The killer probably wouldn't have had time for that, and the search was big enough already.

And it came up with a lot of hits. Daniel snorted when he saw the list. If only the average airline passenger knew how many ex-cons they flew with, they might never go on another vacation again.

Pickpockets, wife beaters, drunk drivers, it was amazing. No murderers, though.

One name, however, did stand out. Jean-Baptiste Gagneux, 47 years of age, originally from La Rochelle but now living in Paris, had spent seven years on the inside for jewel theft. While that wasn't art, it was in the same category. Stealing jewelry wasn't like stealing cars or stereos. You had to know something about the upper crust of the black market to move that sort of thing.

Daniel brought up his file and while Torsson translated, he grew even more interested.

Gagneux had stolen a collection of antique jewelry from a pawn shop in Lyon. Not only that; he had been charged with numerous other counts of theft—antiquarian books, rare letters from famous people, and paintings.

"Bingo," Daniel muttered. Torsson nodded. They read on.

Other than a pawn shop heist, which had been a clever break-in foiled only because the guy he fenced the jewelry to copped a plea bargain and fingered Gagneux, none of the other charges stuck. While in prison for the jewelry charge, he went through three more trials for theft, including a collection of late medieval French religious paintings; but in each case, he was found innocent for lack of evidence.

His lawyer was a pricey one who Torsson said was famous for getting criminals off the hook, so Monsieur Jean-Baptiste Gagneux obviously had some good money squirreled away.

Gagneux got out of prison four years ago and had been the target of no charges or investigations since then.

He had either retired or gotten more careful.

Daniel voted for more careful. In his experience, professional criminals rarely reformed. Prison was a mere temporary setback in a lifelong career of wrongdoing.

"Do we have a record of where he's living now?" Daniel asked once they had finished looking through Gagneux's criminal file.

"All former convicts have to register their address. One moment," Torsson murmured, tapping away on the computer. "Aha! Here he is, and he's right here in Paris. An apartment in a nice district. He still is making good money somehow."

"No prizes for guessing his source of income. Hold on. I need to call Remi," Daniel pulled out his phone.

"The civilian consultant? Do we really need her along for an arrest?"

Daniel smiled. "I want her to take a look at this guy's apartment. She'll see a lot of things you and I won't see. Besides, if I don't take her along for the arrest, she's going chew me out all the way back to the States."

CHAPTER SIXTEEN

Remi's heart pounded as they approached the imposing stone apartment building in the 6th arrondissement, one of the most expensive neighborhoods on the Left Bank of the River Seine. The 12th century spire of the Abbey of Saint Germain, the city's oldest church, stood just around the corner. The streets were lined with exclusive cafés, restaurants, and boulangeries.

Jean-Baptiste Gagneux had chosen not only an expensive neighborhood, but an appropriate one. The area was filled with art galleries, antique stores, and antiquarian bookshops, all catering to the wealthier end of the collector's market. Remi had come here many times to gaze at the treasures on display. A good student of art explored the galleries as much as they did the museums. Since so many important works ended up in private hands, seeing them in a gallery before they were sold might be the only opportunity to see them at all.

Gagneux's building was a grand edifice of gray stone in the Imperial style, with tall windows and ironwork balconies on each of its five floors. An elderly doorman in burgundy livery and a top hat stood out front.

Torsson showed him his identification and the man's eyes went so wide that for a moment Remi worried he might have a heart attack.

"We are looking for Monsieur Jean-Baptiste Gagneux," the Interpol agent said. "Is he still residing in apartment 311, and is he in?"

"Y-yes, sir. He's in, and he's still in the same apartment."

"Is he alone?"

"As far as I know, sir. He came in an hour ago, alone, and he has not had any visitors since."

"Thank you. Stay at your post and speak nothing of this."

The doorman was so flustered he didn't even ask to see Remi's or Daniel's papers. That was fine by Remi. She didn't want to have to explain, once again, that she was a civilian consultant. They seemed to be second-class citizens in the world of law enforcement.

They walked through a marble front hall past a floor-to-ceiling mirror and beneath a brass chandelier.

Daniel turned to them, "Torsson, take the elevator. We'll take the stairs. I don't think that doorman is going to warn him, but we need to cover both exit routes just in case. Remi, hang back. Art thieves aren't generally dangerous but … " He gave a significant shrug.

Remi bit her lip. Her partner didn't have to finish his sentence. The last art thief they had run into had turned out to be a serial killer. This one might very well be the same. He had already killed twice.

At least she had her pepper spray. France may have been strict on carrying firearms, but at least they gave women the chance to defend themselves.

She put her hand in her pocket to reassure herself it was still there.

"He's in room 311," she told him as they ascended stairs covered in red carpet.

"I know. I heard," Daniel said.

"You speak French?" He hadn't mentioned it.

"A little," he said, looking irritated.

"Who taught you?"

"Let's just focus on the case," Daniel snapped.

Remi fell silent. She had found another sensitive spot. This man had several, and it was impossible to predict what they were since they were all so unusual.

They got to the landing of the third floor just as the elevator pinged down the hall. Torsson came out, an old lady dressed all in black and hunched over a cane coming out after him. He nodded and smiled to her, and she said something before hobbling off down the hall.

The Interpol agent joined them, and they stood pretending to talk until the woman unlocked the door to her apartment and disappeared inside.

Once she did, they walked to apartment 311 and listened at the door. Remi could hear the faint strains of Brahms's Symphony No. 1 in C Minor for a moment before cutting off to an announcer. She felt a tug of nostalgia as she recognized the voice. Gagneux was listening to Radio Classique, her favorite classical station. She missed home and running around on this case had made her forget for the moment just how much she missed it.

This man may be a killer, she reminded herself. *Good taste in music doesn't mean he isn't dangerous.*

She put her hand around the little bottle of pepper spray in her pocket.

Daniel gestured for her to step away from the door. She got out of the firing line. Just because guns were illegal didn't mean an international thief wouldn't have one. Daniel stepped out of the way too. Torsson knocked on the door.

After a moment, a man's voice called from inside. "Who is it?"

"Delivery for Monsieur Gagneux," Torsson said. "From Shakespeare and Company."

Remi suppressed a smile. The city's most famous bookshop attracted all resident foreigners. It would be an unlikely destination for one such as Gagneux, however. The Interpol agent should have consulted her.

The sound of movement within. A bolt slid back, and the door opened a little, held by a chain. A frowning face appeared in the narrow space. Remi caught a glimpse of blue eyes and swept back, thinning blonde hair, and muscular shoulders.

"I didn't order … oh!"

Gagneux had spotted there were three people outside his door and not just one.

"Interpol, unlock the—"

Gagneux slammed the door shut. The bolt slid home with a loud click.

Torsson cursed, backed up, and smashed into the door. It shook in its frame and a thin crack appeared in the wood, but it did not break.

Daniel joined him and they rammed into it together. This time the door frame splintered, and Daniel was able to wrench the door open, the chain and bolt falling free from the weakened frame.

The two men rushed inside.

"Freeze! You're under arrest," Torsson shouted. "Hey! Get down from there."

Remi hesitated. She was supposed to stay in the hallway, but curiosity and excitement got the better of her.

She peeked around the shattered door frame.

Past a short entry hallway, with a marble side table and 19th century bronze statue of Artemis, was a sumptuous living room with modern furniture and many fine paintings on the wall. Of more immediate interest, even to an art historian, was the blonde Frenchman clambering over the ironwork railing of the balcony.

They were on the third floor. Gagneux didn't mean to kill himself, did he?

Daniel and Torsson were obviously worried that he might, since they tried to grab him before he went over.

Too late.

The man dropped.

Remi screamed and rushed over with the two law officers to look over the balcony. She didn't know why she did that. She didn't want to see the thief lying broken in the street, but she couldn't resist. Events seemed to push her forward.

But instead of seeing Jean-Baptiste Gagneux lying dead on the pavement, they saw him on the next balcony down.

So did the resident of that apartment, who let out a tremendous squawk.

Gagneux gave a little bow, climbed over the railing, and swung himself down to the next balcony below. While well into his forties, the jewel thief was as fit as a man half his age.

Daniel cursed and rushed out of the apartment, followed closely by Torsson and Remi.

They flew past the old woman with the cane, who had just emerged from her apartment to find out what all the fuss was about and ran down the stairs.

By the time they burst out of the front door, Torsson was well in the lead with Remi a bit behind and Daniel huffing and puffing in the rear.

McDonald's is taking its toll, Remi thought.

Once outside, they looked around. No sign of Gagneux.

The street ran for far enough in either direction for them to tell that Gagneux had gone down one of the four side streets. Torsson ran for one that had a sign indicating a Metro station was in that direction. He pointed to another street and shouted for Daniel to take it. That way, Remi knew, lay the Pont des Arts, a crowded pedestrian bridge across the Seine.

Both were obvious directions to run, but Remi knew the 6th arrondissement well enough to see that another street might be the one Gagneux had chosen. There were two other streets branching off this one. The nearest stopped at a dead end and all the buildings were private apartments. Not a good place to run. The fourth street, however, was a narrow lane running past a popular movie theater flanked by two cafés. There was always a crowd outside. The thief could lose himself in the congestion or even duck into the movie theater.

Remi ran in that direction.

It only took a few seconds to make it to the corner. She hurried around it and nearly slammed into a middle-aged couple walking arm in arm.

She gasped out an apology, ignored a rude comment from the woman, and ran around them.

And stopped in despair.

The movie theater was just letting out. A big crowd of people spread out on the sidewalk and street, people moving in both directions or standing in small groups, talking. The nearest café was full. She couldn't even see the second café beyond the theater. The crowd was that thick.

I've lost him, she thought in despair.

No! If you lose him, more people will die.

Remi ran into the crowd, weaving between people who chattered away on phones or talked with their partners about the film they had just seen as if nothing strange was going on around them.

The mob of complacent, unaware people seemed endless. Remi grew frustrated as she tried to search through the thickening throng. Didn't these people know danger lurked right in their midst? Was this teenager taking a selfie and blocking her path so asleep they couldn't understand her urgency? Now she understood her father's constant dinner table complaints about "civilians." People went through their lives as sleepwalkers.

She had too, of course. Not too long ago, she had been one of these clueless, complacent people.

Now she saw the world as it really was, and it thrilled and terrified her in equal measure.

There! She could just see a blonde head and a pair of burly shoulders moving through the far side of the crowd.

Jean-Baptiste Gagneux walked quickly, but he did not run. He did not want to cause a visible stir in the crowd. He also didn't look back, as the face is more recognizable than the back of the head.

I'm beginning to think like a criminal.

Remi wasn't sure how she felt about that. At least she had tracked down Gagneux. She didn't have time to pull out her phone. In fact, she didn't even think to.

So now I'm about to confront a murderer. Alone. What did Daniel say about that?

She forged ahead, trying to catch up with the suspect.

They emerged from the crowd at almost the same time. As they did, both picked up their pace. Remi pulled the pepper spray from her pocket, ran to close the last distance between them, and cut him off, holding up the pepper spray and aiming it at his face.

Gagneux stopped. A moment's confusion flickered on his face before he recognized Remi.

"Out of my way!"

Suddenly aware of her position, Remi took a step back. Somebody cried out. People moved away from them.

"Make a move and I'll spray you in the eyes," she warned Gagneux.

The art thief looked to either side, then back at Remi, balling his fists.

"Are you an officer of the law?" he demanded.

Remi smiled. "No, but he is."

Just then, Daniel tackled Gagneux from behind. Both men went down. Gagneux struggled, but while he was more fit than Daniel, the FBI agent had caught him by surprise and was on top. By the time he recovered from his shock, the handcuffs were already around one wrist.

"Jean-Baptiste Gagneux, I presume you speak English. I'm arresting you for the murder of Montgomery Dyson and Pierre Lafontaine."

Gagneux bucked like a bronco in those Westerns that Remi's father always liked to watch, but Daniel straddled him like a cowboy and didn't fall off. Next Gagneux elbowed him. Daniel let out a grunt, gave the suspect an angry kidney punch, and handcuffed the other wrist.

"I'll add resisting arrest and assaulting an officer of the law to those charges," Daniel told him.

"Get off me, American pig!"

"Oink, oink," Daniel said, hauling him to his feet.

"Good job," Remi said, putting her pepper spray back in her pocket. "I thought you went down the other street."

Daniel waved his arm at the staring crowd. "Clear out! Make room!" Then he turned to Remi and smiled. "When I saw you run off in another direction, I figured you knew something we didn't. Guess my hunch paid off, huh?"

Remi smiled back at him. "And so did mine."

CHAPTER SEVENTEEN

Remi discovered that interrogation rooms in French police stations were almost exactly the same as those in American police stations.

They had the same bare concrete interiors, the same metal desk and chairs bolted to the floor, the same security cameras, and the same one-way mirror along one wall.

The difference this time was that she was on the interesting side of that one-way mirror, not stuck in the observation room. She wasn't simply watching the interrogation; she got to be part of it.

She and Torsson sat opposite Jean-Baptiste Gagneux, who sat slumped and sullen, handcuffed to his chair. Daniel paced back and forth behind him.

For a moment, everyone was silent. Remi felt the actual law officers should take the lead. Torsson had done nothing except bring Gagneux a cup of coffee. All Daniel was doing was pacing back and forth, cursing quietly to himself.

Then suddenly he dove in close to Gagneux and shouted in his ear, "Two men dead! Two men dead for a couple of paintings? What's the matter with you? Are you insane?"

Remi studied Gagneux's face. He did not react to the insane comment. The mad hated being called mad.

No, he didn't seem angry, or unbalanced.

He did look worried, though.

"A murder in France and a murder in New York," Daniel went on. "Sure, here they'll put you in some comfy cell with color TV and croissants, but in New York you'll be the girlfriend of some 300-pound meth dealer named Bubba. At least before they fry your ass."

Remi didn't think there was still a death penalty in New York, but saw no reason to inform Gagneux of that.

Torsson leaned forward. "You don't seem like a killer to me. But we need to clear this up. You flew from New York to Paris just in time to be in both locations for the murders."

"Coincidence," Gagneux muttered.

"Oh yeah?" Daniel bellowed. "Then why did you run?"

Gagneux didn't answer.

"Why don't you tell us why you ran?" Torsson said gently. "Were you scared because of your criminal record?"

This was a game Remi had learned was called "good cop, bad cop." Daniel was playing the bad cop, an obvious role after that kidney punch. The object of the game was for the suspect to fear the bad cop and look to the good cop for help.

It worked.

Gagneux nodded.

Daniel leaned in closer, whispering into his ear. "You'll serve a term here and a term in New York. You'll never see the light of day again."

"I didn't do it."

"Where are the paintings?"

"I didn't do it!"

Daniel slapped his palm against the metal table with a loud bang.

"You were present in New York and Paris at the right times. You are an art thief. You had the knowledge, the opportunity, and the motive. And you ran. Only guilty people run."

Gagneux looked at the floor, lips moving silently. He appeared to be thinking.

"Two counts of murder is a very serious charge," Torsson said. "If you have another explanation, you better come clean with it."

Gagneux thought for a moment more, heaved a big sigh, and looked at Torsson. "Are the police still searching my apartment?"

"Yes."

"Have them pull aside the bureau in my bedroom. They'll find a loose pancl in thc wall. Opcn that and you'll find a bag of pcarl necklaces. If you contact the MacPhearson family of Mt. Kisco, New York, you'll find they were stolen a few days ago."

Torsson got on the phone to the search team. Daniel pulled out his phone too. As the FBI agent tapped away at it, he walked over to Torsson and Remi's side of the table and showed them his screen. He was on a New York state database of open cases. Searching under Mt. Kisco, a town Remi had never heard of, he found that Robert and Shella MacPhearson had reported the theft of several strings of pearls of a total value of $100,000 from their house the very same day Montgomery Dyson got scythed in the East Gallery of his mansion in the Hamptons.

Remi pulled out her own phone and checked on Google Maps to see the driving time between Mt. Kisco and East Hampton. Almost three hours. It was virtually impossible that Gagneux could have committed both crimes in the same night.

Remi groaned and sat back. They had been too eager. While Gagneux was an art thief who was in the right state at the right time, he wasn't a perfect match. He had no history of violence and no connection to the paintings other than the fact that he had been accused of stealing art in the past.

They had been so desperate to catch the killer before he struck again, they had just given the killer more time.

Torsson put away his phone, a sour look on his face. "They searched behind the bureau and found the pearls."

"Damn it!" Daniel shouted. "We keep solving the wrong damn crimes!"

Remi looked from her partner to Gagneux and back. Another dead end.

* * *

In the hall outside the interrogation room, Daniel paced back and forth. They had decided to take a break. Gagneux was still in the interrogation room. They'd question him a bit more later, although there didn't seem much point. He looked like he was an innocent man.

Well, innocent of the murders, anyway.

And now they were stuck at a dead end, and he had just received an email from Assistant Director Ochiai asking for a progress report. Maybe he wouldn't send a report since there was no progress.

Damn it! He'd never get back to the Behavioral Affairs Unit at this rate.

Although it looked like the Behavioral Affairs Unit had followed him. This had all the makings of a serial murder. The guy had killed twice in two creative ways and would probably do so again. Remi was right, he was collecting the paintings. The question was—how many more did he need? There was no record of one of the previous owners being killed for it. They'd have found out about that already. So did the killer need to kill for two more paintings, or did he already obtain one or two by more honest means?

If he already had the complete set, he might go to ground, and they'd never find him.

Daniel couldn't let someone like that get off the hook. He prided himself on always getting his man.

And if he didn't get this man, not only would a killer go free, but Daniel's career would be on the ropes. He had already been demoted to this Podunk division as punishment for being a bit too "assertive" in his handling of suspects, and for talking back to his superiors. If he couldn't produce results, consistently and quickly, he'd end up as a filing clerk at Quantico.

And then there was this place …

The cafés, the architecture, the sound of the language, it all reminded him of when he was a kid.

Ever since his trips with his mother and "Uncle" Ray, he'd avoided going to Europe. His ex-wife had nagged him about coming here. "You know so much; why don't you want to go back?" He kept his silence and insisted on going to Mexico instead.

Uncle Ray had never taken him to Mexico. He hadn't been interested in Latin America.

He sure had been interested in young Daniel, though.

Mom had been an academic, spending more time in museums and archives than with her son. She always had an excuse for disappearing into some dusty old place for a whole afternoon.

"Not a problem," Uncle Ray would tell her, putting an arm around Daniel, who would plaster on a smile and try not to squirm. "We'll keep ourselves entertained with guy stuff."

Daniel shuddered. All over Europe—France, Germany, Italy, the Low Countries—it had been the same. Mom ditching him and Uncle Ray wanting to do "guy stuff."

The sound of Torsson running up to him snapped him out of his reverie. The Swede was waving his phone, his eyes lit up. "I've got it! I know where Pestilence is."

"That was quick."

The Interpol agent had only set someone on that task a few hours before.

"It has only been sold three times in the past forty years, first to a private buyer right here in Paris who died a few years later. Then to a buyer in Rome, an ex-member of the Opus Dei in Rome, some defrocked priest who got kicked out of the church for performing what were called Satanic rites. It was a bit of a scandal. He just died and it was sold on to Pier Paolo Manetti in Florence."

Torsson said this like he expected Daniel to know who he was talking about.

"Who?"

Torsson looked surprised. "Pier Paolo Manetti? *Misterio 2000*?"

"Nope."

"It was a hugely popular television show. I know it made it to America."

"I don't watch much TV. You can't catch serial killers that way."

Torsson shook his head. "Don't you ever stop working?"

"Not really, no." *What else would I do with myself?*

"You have to take time off, you know."

"Don't start talking like my ex-wife," Daniel snapped. When he saw the Swede's expression, he continued in a more level tone. "Try to get us on a plane as soon as possible. There must be plenty of flights between Paris and Florence. We'll grab Remi and you can tell me all about this guy on the way to the airport."

"You think he's the murderer?"

"Or a potential victim."

"Maybe we should warn him."

"If we warn him and he's the murderer, we'll lose him."

"But if he's the next victim …"

Daniel thought a moment. "You only found out this guy has the painting of Pestilence by using a court order to see sales records. It's unlikely our killer has the same access. He's obviously good at tracing these paintings, but chances are he won't be able to find the location as quickly as your team did. On the other hand, he might. How about this—we don't tell this TV show guy, but we inform the Italian police and have them keep an eye on him."

"All right," Torsson said with a nod, already getting on his phone. "I'll give them a call and then get us the first plane out."

CHAPTER EIGHTEEN

Pier Paolo Manetti looked even more like an opera star in real life than he did on television.

The Fifth Horseman watched him from across the restaurant in Florence, a short, portly man with deep laughter lines, curly black hair that was almost certainly dyed, and a jovial round face that smiled and smacked contentedly as he dug into a generous helping of pasta.

Manetti looked older and stouter than he had on his famous television show, *Misterio 2000*, but it was undoubtedly him. There was no mistaking those exaggerated mannerisms, that crazily unkempt hair that somehow managed to give him style, or that waxed moustache that came out to points on either end, nearly doubling the width of his already wide face.

There couldn't be two of those moustaches anywhere, not even in Italy.

So the Fifth Horseman watched, and waited. He enjoyed every bite of Manetti's meal almost as much as the Italian himself. He would also enjoy watching the result of that meal when it kicked in about an hour from now.

As embarrassing as it was to admit to himself, *Misterio 2000* was one of the shows that had set the Fifth Horsemen on this path.

It was a ridiculous program, begun, as the name implied, during the wave of paranormal interest around the turn of the millennium. Filmed in Italian for Italian TV, it was soon an international hit for the elaborate gestures and mannerisms of its host. It was the only Italian show on American network television, and they didn't even dub it, instead opting for subtitles so viewers wouldn't miss Manetti's extravagant mode of speech and occasional bursts into song.

Manetti and his program became a cult hit, but while most people only watched it for laughs, the Fifth Horseman noticed a more serious side to the show that the general public missed. Manetti researched his topics in depth, and while he never lost his showman's façade, he conducted informative interviews with UFO abductees, conspiracy theorists, and people who claimed to have lived past lives.

Manetti was at his most serious when speaking of the mysteries related to the Christian religion. On one program he even went all the way to Axum in Ethiopia, where church elders claimed to keep the original Ark of the Covenant hidden in the sanctum sanctorum of the great Ethiopian Orthodox Church there. Only the eyes of the clergy were allowed to gaze on it.

Manetti broke into the church one night, nearly got shot by a guard, and was arrested by Ethiopian police. His eventual release, and the smuggling out of the footage, created an international incident and hugely entertaining television.

It was that episode that made the Fifth Horseman realize Manetti was something more than a showman. He really wanted answers, and was willing to put his freedom, even his life, on the line in order to get them.

A man after his own heart.

But a rival. And rivals needed to be dealt with, each in their own special way.

The Fifth Horseman ate his *crespelle alla Fiorentina* and bided his time.

After a second portion and a generous helping of gelato for dessert, Manetti lifted himself off his seat with a grunt, paid the bill, and left.

The Fifth Horseman, who had been nursing a glass of wine to pass the time, drained it and quickly paid.

Manetti huffed down the Via Sant'Antonino, singing a popular love song in his trademark baritone. His voice echoed off the crumbling old buildings on either side of the narrow street, the flaking tan paint and worn green shutters somehow seeming attractive and homey despite their modest nature.

A gray-haired woman leaned out of a third-story window and clapped.

"Bravo! Bravo, Signore Manetti!"

Ever the entertainer, Manetti stopped and sang the rest of the song below her window like some ardent young lover in a cheap Italian romance film from the fifties. The woman put her chin on her crossed arms and listened, beaming with delight from the attention.

Once done, Manetti bowed, got another round of applause from several people who had appeared at their windows, and moved on, starting up a new song.

No one noticed the Fifth Horseman walking half a block behind him.

Still singing, Manetti continued into the Piazza di Santa Maria Novella whose famous Renaissance basilica of the same name made it the epicenter of tourism.

The TV star strode right across the piazza, singing as he went past the ornate basilica façade of white marble with its perfectly proportioned arches. Tourists turned and started taking pictures.

The Fifth Horseman slowed, putting more distance between him and his quarry. While he was only a face in the crowd, he knew the police would soon be studying those pictures. There were already dozens of photos of him in a suit of armor.

He wondered how well the police would be able to trace it. The armor and sword were modern reproductions, purchased in Germany ten years before.

The Fifth Horseman had been planning these encounters with the paintings' owners long before he knew who his intended victims were.

While he had paid in cash, there weren't many modern armorers who could make a suit of such quality. The authorities might be able to narrow it down. Briefly he considered flying to Germany and killing the craftsman but discarded the idea almost as soon as he thought of it. That would only bring attention to where the armor came from, and he didn't have time to take a side trip anyway.

No, he had far, far more important things to do.

He needed to see the stars in all four paintings. Only then could he know the time.

And the time was everything.

Manetti's belting song cut off as the man coughed, tapped his chest, and continued walking, a bit slower now. He took up the next verse with a little less gusto than before.

Passing through the piazza, Manetti turned onto the Via del Banchi. A few steps into the new street, his song was interrupted by a loud belch.

Manetti stopped, cleared his throat, thumped his chest, and continued. His pace grew even slower, and he did not sing.

That gave the Fifth Horsemen time to duck into the recessed arched doorway of a villa and make a quick change. From out of his pocket came a burlap bag from which he pulled a small mirror and makeup kit.

Putting those on the ground, he shucked off his jacket and tie and slacks to reveal a second set of clothes beneath.

These were not nearly so formal. A loose white blouse of medieval style and brown britches with a belt and a big square buckle. The sort of clothes someone of modest means would have worn five hundred years ago. Dirty and torn as well and stained here and there with blood. A large red stain ran down the front of the shirt, as if he had vomited up blood.

The Fifth Horseman opened the makeup kit and quickly daubed a sponge into some yellow base and covered his hands and face with it to give him a sickly pallor. Then he used a small brush and some red paint to dab little spots all over his exposed skin. A quick look in the mirror showed him he had done a satisfactory job.

He had practiced this change of costume a hundred times. Every move was quick and assured and he barely even needed the mirror to guide his hand. Within less than a minute he was done and, with the sackcloth bag slung over his shoulder, he stepped out of the doorway and saw Manetti had only made it a further half-block down the street.

The Fifth Horseman followed at a discreet distance, smiling. A few people gave him and his strange getup a second glance, but no one stared for too long. They no doubt thought he was going to a fancy-dress party or was an actor in one of Florence's many outdoor entertainments.

Strange costumes were common on the streets. Just today, he had passed a woman dressed up as Lucrezia Borgia, a man imitating Michelangelo, a trio of condottieri, and a woman in Roman robes covered from head to toe in marble colored makeup in order to imitate a statue.

The Fifth Horseman and his quarry continued down Via del Banchi, another of Florence's narrow residential streets enclosed by four- or five-story apartment buildings on either side, with a few shops on the ground floors and many windows overlooking the street. The Fifth Horseman knew that Manetti loved singing along these little lanes, loved the sound of his own voice; but the Fifth Horseman also knew that Manetti wasn't feeling quite himself today.

Yes, a bit under the weather. Perhaps it was something he ate.

At an intersection about a hundred yards down the street, where the Via del Giglio branched off at an angle, stood a small, whitewashed palazzo. Its wall sported an ornate crest of some old Florentine family and a ponderous door of thick wood studded with brass.

Manetti's home. Pulling open that door made the television personality break into a sweat.

The Fifth Horseman hurried up to him just as he managed to get it open.

"Signor Manetti," the Fifth Horseman said in passable Italian. "You look unwell. Do you need some help?"

The TV star's round face shone with sweat, and his breath smelled distinctly unpleasant. He looked at the newcomer in his strange outfit, confused.

"I'm sorry, do I know you?"

"No, but I know you. I am one of your greatest fans. I'm an astrologer."

Manetti's bushy eyebrows shot up. "An astrologer? Ah, perhaps you can help me after all! Dressed as you are, I thought you were a street entertainer, or maybe a portent of death like might appear in an opera by Puccini. You are right, I am feeling a bit poorly. Help me up the stairs and get me a glass of water, and I will show you something more astounding than anything I ever put on television."

The Fifth Horseman closed the door behind them, the heavy thud resounding in the front hall, then snicked the bolt shut. With Manetti leaning on his arm, his other hand grasping a smooth old balustrade, the Fifth Horsemen led him up a flight of worn stone steps. They passed through another door and into a hallway that branched right and also continued forward. Manetti gestured forward with a groan and the Fifth Horseman took him down the passage and into high-ceilinged sitting room. A gilded loveseat and a couple of armchairs were arranged around a coffee table strewn with books on the occult and paranormal events. A long bookcase filled with similar books took up one wall.

While all the shutters were closed to block out the heat of the noonday sun and the Fifth Horseman couldn't read the titles from across the room, he could have named most of them. Any time Manetti mentioned a book in one of his shows, the Fifth Horseman bought it and pored over its contents.

And he wasn't really interested in the books right now anyway. He was far more interested in the easel and painting covered with a cloth in the opposite corner of the room.

The TV host sat heavily in one of the armchairs.

“Please,” he choked, loosening his collar. “A glass of water. The kitchen is just down that hall.”

The Fifth Horsemen went to fetch him a glass of water. It didn’t matter. It would do Manetti no good.

When he returned a minute later, he found Manetti where he had left him, sweat pouring down his face.

“Thank you, my good man,” Manetti gasped.

Manetti took the glass gratefully and downed it in one gulp. Then he winced, clutched his stomach, and let out a foul belch.

“Do forgive me. I seemed to have a touch of food poisoning. I can’t imagine how. I’ve been eating at Marco’s for years and have always had excellent service.”

“A rare seasoning perhaps, added by a novice chef.”

“Perhaps,” Manetti set the glass on an inlaid side table. “Now, my astrologer friend, let me show you something as a reward for your kindness. Go uncover that painting over there and open the shutter a bit so you can see it better.”

The Fifth Horseman strode across the room, excitement rising in him. He opened the shutter a crack, just enough to let in light but not enough for the neighbors across the street to see inside. Then he went to the easel and carefully removed the cloth, his hands trembling a little.

He stood staring for a moment, the cloth hanging from his hand like a miniature ghost.

“A painting of Pestilence, one of the Four Horsemen of the Apocalypse,” the Fifth Horseman said, his voice almost stilled with awe. The third out of four.

“Ah! So you are familiar with medieval symbolism.”

“You might say those four are old friends.”

“Tell me, my good astrologer, what do you make of this painting?”

“You mean of the figure pointing to the tavern sign?”

“Yes! Yes! Oh, you saw it immediately. One of the great blessings in my life has been my fans. So many have interesting fields of study. So many see what the mundane world does not want us to see.”

The Fifth Horseman could not help but feel flattered at the praise from one of his former idols. He almost regretted what he had done and what he would continue to do.

But he held firm. The work was too important.

"I see the constellation Lyra, the harp," the Fifth Horseman replied. "A fitting constellation to name a tavern after. One of the musicians lying dead on the ground even has a harp to emphasize the symbolism."

"Quite true. You have a good eye, my friend. I'm sorry, I didn't catch your name?"

The Fifth Horseman ignored that question. Instead, he asked one of his own.

"You are an expert in the occult and the paranormal. Unlike many who watch your show, I can see beyond your showmanship, your singing and your amusing antics. You are not some cheap entertainer. You are wise in the ways of the hidden world. Tell me, what does this painting mean?"

Manetti wiped his brow, his breathing coming in gasps. He looked like he wanted to lie down but was so excited by having a receptive audience for his painting that he kept talking.

"The key to everything! The secrets of the universe are hidden in this painting. As you might have guessed, there are three others to make a set, showing all Four Horsemen of the Apocalypse. I only have this one so far, sadly. Even so, it has taught me so very much. Each of the four paintings is a piece of the puzzle, but each part tells you more and more the longer you look at it. The constellation Lyra symbolizes the music of the spheres, the great concert that God set in motion to give order to the universe."

"What?" the Fifth Horseman exclaimed, stricken with disappointment. Was Manetti serious, or was he simply playing him for a fool?

Manetti leaned forward, eager to make his point, but clutched his stomach, winced, and leaned back again. With a voice even weaker than before, he continued.

"The universe is like a great symphony, ordered and beautiful. It is constrained by certain rules, like music, and like music its individual parts, its individual notes, mean nothing without the others. All act to create a whole, and the final meaning isn't clear until the symphony is finished. Nothing makes sense until the apocalypse."

"And when will that be?" the Fifth Horseman asked, impatient.

Manetti managed a little shrug, then belched. "When do we know a symphony is finished? Only when it is. Oh, we can see signs it's coming to a crescendo, and those signs are there, my friend, but we can't really know until it's all over."

The Fifth Horseman groaned. Maybe Manetti was more of a showman than he had thought.

He shook his head, rage mounting in him. He took several deep breaths, staring at the painting, then turned on the TV host, his eyes afire. "All your research, Manetti, all your interviews with great thinkers, and you're still as ignorant as most of your viewers."

The TV show host blinked. "I beg your pardon?"

"You have missed the point, you overly mustached ignoramus. The whole purpose of these paintings is to tell us when it will happen. The mayor of Haarlem discovered the date of the apocalypse, along with his inner circle of freemason associates. He ordered the paintings made as a step-by-step guide to knowing the fate of the world, a sort of instruction manual for those who have gone beyond the initiation stage. That's why you need all four paintings. You can't get anything from one part of the four, because you need all four to cast a horoscope. Then we'll know the precise date of the end of the world. And there's no music of the spheres, no grand symphony. It's all chaos descending into more chaos."

Manetti stared, trembling from more than the poison in his veins. He seemed to take in the Fifth Horseman's costume with new understanding. "Wh-who are you?"

The Fifth Horseman looked him in the eye. "Your murderer. You don't deserve the painting, and you don't deserve the wisdom it contains. I thought you'd be the closest to the truth out of all of them. It turns out you're the furthest. I'm glad I poisoned your food."

Manetti looked at him in panic, clutching his belly protectively. "Poisoned my food?"

The Fifth Horseman gave him a grim smile. "Not as fitting a death as the others, but I couldn't get my hands on any anthrax. Even my wealth and connections can only go so far."

"You poisoned me?" Manetti asked, doubling over as another cramp hit him.

"Yes, and now I'm going to take your painting."

The Fifth Horseman turned to the painting, threw the cloth over it, and lifted it off the easel.

"No!" Manetti cried.

He tried to rise, only to fall on his knees. As the Fifth Horseman walked casually out across the room, Manetti crawled after him, gasping for breath.

Pier Paolo Manetti, famous worldwide for his show *Misterio 2000*, only made it a few feet before he heaved out the contents of his stomach, gurgled, and fell face first into a pool of his own vomit, stone dead.

CHAPTER NINETEEN

Four hours later, they landed in Florence, Remi rubbing her eyes with exhaustion. She should have snatched some sleep on the plane, but she had been too excited. They were closing in on the killerl she could feel it.

Even better, by a lucky coincidence, the purchaser of Pestilence lived in the very same city that housed the archives for the archaeological excavation of the Church of Saint Pantaleon of Nicomedia, the church marked on the map hidden inside the cryptex. Perhaps she'd find the time to duck into the archives in the middle of the investigation.

Perhaps? No, she *must* find the time.

Luckily, they had been able to get to Florence quickly. Torsson had to flash his badge to get them onto a flight that was just departing Paris. Now they headed for the taxi stand just outside the terminal so they could go to the home of Pier Paolo Manetti, the famous Italian TV host. Torsson had gotten his address from the bill of sale.

As soon as they got off the plane, the Interpol agent had called the Florentine police to ask for a situation report. They had informed him that Manetti was lunching at his usual restaurant, a place not far from his house called Marco's. They sent him the address and said that if he followed his usual pattern, he'd go home after lunch.

"Good," Torsson said, speaking passable Italian. "Give us the number of the man you have on him."

Remi watched as Torsson's face hardened. "What? This is important. I know you have other work but … well get him back as quickly as you can."

He hung up and turned to Remi and Daniel.

"They only have a man on him part-time. They're overstretched. Apparently, they're following some terror suspects as well. Several Iraqis and Syrians on the watch list have come to Florence in the past couple of days. And they have most of their remaining plainclothes officers in the major crowds because it's tourist season."

"This is Florence," Remi objected. "It's always tourist season."

Torsson shrugged.

"Do you think the terror suspects might be linked to the painting?" Remi asked.

"I doubt it. We haven't found any connections like that so far. Come on," Daniel said impatiently, heading for the taxi stand. "Let's get to him as quick as we can."

They hurried out of the airport and grabbed a taxi. As Remi sat in the back seat, she looked out the window with an eagerness bordering on glee. Not only were they close on the trail of the murderer—whether it turned out to be Manetti or not—but they were now in the same city where the archives were for the church she needed to explore.

Perfect.

The murder first, she reminded herself. *Those archives aren't going anywhere.*

Remi tried to focus on the case, thinking through what they knew so far.

Remi had actually spoken with Manetti once on the phone a couple of years ago. He had been preparing a show on the cryptex and other medieval mysteries and wanted her as a guest.

"Aren't you the fellow who talks with people who claim to be lizard aliens?" she had asked.

"Oh, you saw that episode? Do you think there might be a connection between the invaders from the constellation Draco and the cryptex?"

She had hung up.

Now she had to meet this idiot in person.

Idiot, yes, but a useful idiot. The fact that he had purchased the painting for 180,000 euros showed he had a serious interest in it, and that he thought it held some deep occult truth.

That confirmed Remi's gut feeling that the stars in each painting had some sort of significance. Perhaps they linked together to spell out a message or code.

The killer obviously thought so. He obviously wanted to collect all four.

Sitting in the taxi from the airport with the two lawmen, Remi had a horrible thought. What if the killer already had one of the paintings before he started the killing spree? Maybe he only needed to get this one final painting to achieve his goal?

Would that stop the killings, or only lead to a mass slaughter? What was the killer building up to?

"Daniel, what do you think the killer is after?" she asked. "What would a man obsessed with the Apocalypse want?"

Daniel, sitting next to her, grimaced. "Nothing good. He got really showy in the way he killed his first two victims." Remi shuddered at the way he said this, assuming, like her, that there would be more. "I think he wants to strike out in self-destructive nihilism. Like school shooters. They want to die like your regular teen suicide case, but they're different because they want to take a bunch of people with them. Your usual teen suicide shows hatred for themselves. School shooters hate themselves and everyone else. They want to prove to the world that nothing matters."

"So this is what we're facing," Remi murmured.

"It's just a theory, but yeah. That's what my gut tells me."

"Your 'gut' and mine agree," Remi said and sighed.

Torsson, sitting next to the driver, glanced at them through the rearview mirror.

"You've hunted serial killers before?" he asked.

Daniel gave him a bitter smile. "Me, plenty of times. This is only her second."

The Swede looked shocked. "I've been an officer for almost fifteen years and never tackled a serial killer case."

"They rarely go international," Daniel explained. "Sometimes the perpetrators don't have the means or the self-control. More often they're simply creatures of habit, staying within a well-known region to commit their crimes."

"Except this one," Torsson said.

"Lucky us," Daniel replied with false delight. "Although our man might not fit the exact definition of a serial killer, at least not yet. He wants the paintings and has some sort of grudge against those who own them. Remi here thinks they have occult symbolism, so maybe he sees the legal owners as rivals in the spellcasting business. And yes, I do think he's going to escalate. No one goes around bumping people off who don't need to be and then suddenly throws up his hands, shouts 'I'm done,' and retires to Florida."

Torsson nodded. "I'll need to liaise with the local Interpol office. Set up the practicalities of our investigation here. It's not far from the highway into the city. I'll have the driver drop me off there and you can proceed to Manetti's home."

"But we're going to Manetti's right now!" Daniel objected.

Torsson shrugged. "Orders are orders. I'm sure you have bureaucracy in the FBI too."

"We sure do," Daniel grumbled. "But can't you wait a couple of hours?"

"No, unfortunately I can't. We have to check in immediately after we get to a new country. International law. Do you speak Italian?"

"I speak American," Daniel grumbled.

And some French you don't want to admit, Remi thought.

Torsson got on his phone. "I'll send Remi the name and number of the plainclothes officer who has been assigned to Manetti. Unfortunately, he just went off duty. He said he'd check on the suspect in half an hour."

"We'll get there first," Remi said.

Torsson gave them a bitter smile. "Italian police are not the most efficient in the world. I can tell what they're thinking: that a famous and slightly ridiculous TV personality couldn't be a murderer, and that he wouldn't be a target of a murderer in broad daylight since he's so well-known. They are very good at rationalizing ways to not do their job. They did promise to watch his house all night, and I think they will actually do that."

"We'll have solved this by then," Remi objected.

"Maybe, maybe not," Daniel said. "All right. Go do your paperwork and join us as quick as you can."

The taxi took a diversion into an office suburb with glass and steel buildings that spoke of none of the beauty for which Florence was famous. Leaving Torsson in front of a nondescript office with only a small sign to announce the presence of the world's most important international law organization, Daniel and Remi proceeded to the center of town.

As they did, the matchless skyline of one of the world's most beautiful cities came into view. Remi had seen it many times, and yet every time it lifted her heart and took her breath away.

They passed along a bridge spanning the Arno River, its banks lined with elegant old palazzos of stone that shone red in the brilliant Italian light. Beyond rose the marble and brick domes of the city's great churches, and the solid spires of various towers erected by the great families of the Renaissance both as artistic statements and for defense. They did not rise as high as the famous ones in Bologna, as if their owners did not want to mar the exquisite skyline of their city.

Those towers had been necessary, Remi remembered, for as much as Renaissance Florence had been a center of art and learning, it had also been a whirlwind of backstabbing politics and intrigue. Back in those days, the lovely streets had been washed in blood.

And if they didn't hurry, they would be again.

"Should we have called ahead to Manetti?" Remi wondered.

"We went through this," Daniel replied. "If Manetti is the killer, we'd only end up warning him."

"I suppose," Remi said, fidgeting. "And it's doubtful the killer could have learned about the sale and gotten here so quickly after Paris."

"Right. He'd have to stash the painting, ditch that ridiculous King Arthur getup, and get here unobtrusively. Not something you can easily do in just a couple of days. Then, of course, he'd have to track down Manetti. We'll question the guy and if we're satisfied that he isn't guilty, we'll put him under police protection. I hope the cops here are better than their army."

"What's that supposed to mean?"

Daniel snorted. "World War Two."

"They didn't fight so badly."

"Spoken like a true Frenchwoman."

"Oh, God! Typical American. You think you won World War Two all by yourselves, even though you came in two years late."

"Well, we did win it."

"No, the Russians were the ones to break the Germans' back. The only thing the Americans and the other Allies did was to save Western Europe from Communism after the Soviets saved it from fascism."

"You're welcome."

The taxi let them off in front of an old palazzo at the intersection of two narrow side streets. As Daniel paid the driver, Remi stared at the heavy wooden door, her heart pounding. Finally, she would see one of the paintings up close. Finally, she would speak to one of its owners.

Would he have any answers for her? He had seemed like a crank on the phone, and the few snippets of his show Remi had watched had not changed her perception, but he was deep into occultism and conspiracy theories. While all that was simple nonsense, he might have some valuable insights into the nature of the man they hunted.

Unless he was the man they hunted.

They needed to take care.

The taxi drove off, turned a corner, and went out of sight. No one was nearby on this little back street.

Quietly they crossed the street to the heavy wooden door studded with brass. Remi recognized it as 18th or 19th century, an imitation of old medieval portals. It had been a fashion in the early modern period to imitate the glories of the Middle Ages.

Remi was about to ring the worn ivory doorbell when Daniel put a hand on her arm. He nodded toward the door, and she saw it stood slightly ajar.

"Maybe I'm just a paranoid American who never made the world safe for democracy," he whispered, "but I don't think it's normal to leave your front door open."

"No," she whispered back, "not even in Europe."

Putting one hand on the butt of his pistol inside his jacket, Daniel used the other to push the door open. Both of them winced as it made a deep creaking sound.

A flight of worn marble steps led up to an interior door, also open.

Daniel stepped through and pulled out his gun.

"Is this legal?" Remi whispered.

"Not really, no," Daniel whispered back.

Daniel tiptoed up the stairs, motioning for Remi to stay put. She hesitated until he was about halfway up, then followed.

She wasn't about to be left behind, not when they were this close.

Her partner didn't seem to notice her following, because without looking back he got to the top of the landing and disappeared through the door.

Remi got to the landing a few seconds later and found herself in a front hall adorned with engravings of religious subjects and battle scenes. Daniel was heading down a passage to the right. Remi saw a large room ahead to the left and made for it. Splitting up would cover more of the house more quickly.

Creeping down the hall, her footsteps muffled by a worn old carpet, the room slowly came into view. Oil paintings hung on the walls. Ornate Empire style side tables held antique clocks and delicate porcelain.

After another few steps, the entire room came into view.

Remi stopped short, frozen with fear.

A rotund little man lay face down in a pool of vomit, not moving. Another man, dressed in a bathrobe and slippers, stood over him.

Remi took a sharp inhalation of breath. The stranger whipped around and saw her.

CHAPTER TWENTY

Remi froze. The man looked in his thirties, with unkempt hair and wild, bloodshot eyes. He had a stocky build and thick, hairy arms.

She felt panic rise up in her. She tried to scream for Daniel, but the words caught in her throat.

But it was the man who backed away first.

"Don't!" he said in the Italian of a native speaker, raising his hands. "Take whatever you want! Just don't kill me."

Remi blinked, unsure of herself. The Italian paused too.

The sound of running feet made him jerk his gaze in the direction from which Remi had come. As Daniel rushed into the room, the man bolted down a side hallway.

Daniel took one look at the man dead on the floor, who Remi now recognized as Pier Paolo Manetti, and took off after him.

Remi shook herself out of her stunned inaction and followed.

The Italian led them down a short hallway to a kitchen. He opened a window above the counter and climbed up to it.

"Oh no!" Daniel shouted. "We've had enough parkour for one case!"

Daniel grabbed him by the leg and hauled him back in. The man hit the counter, rattling the dishes in the drainer, and then landed hard on the tiled floor. His bathrobe flapped open, and Remi got an unwelcome view of a white pot belly and dirty underwear.

"Don't kill me! Don't kill me!" the man said, waving his arms and legs in the air like an overturned cockroach.

"What's he saying?" Daniel asked as he flipped him over and pulled out the cuffs.

"He's saying for you not to kill him."

"That's rich, coming from someone like him."

Remi watched as Daniel slapped the cuffs on and helped the man up. The prisoner trembled all over.

"We're not going to kill you," Remi told the prisoner. "This is Daniel Walker of the Federal Bureau of Investigation. I'm Remi

Laurent, his civilian advisor. He is detaining you on suspicion of murder."

"I didn't kill Pier Paolo!"

"What are you doing here?" Remi demanded.

"I'm a house guest. I'm staying with Pier Paolo to advise him on a documentary series he's filming."

"On what?"

"Astrology."

Remi blinked. That was interesting.

Daniel looked at her. "Um, translation please?"

"He says he's a house guest helping Manetti with a documentary on astrology. He says he's innocent."

"Don't they all," Daniel studied him a moment. "You speak English?"

The man shook his head and said in slow, heavily accented English. "No, I speak very little of the English."

"Looks like you get to be translator again," Daniel said. "I told you that you'd be useful on this case."

"I think I was the one who told you."

"Whatever. Ask him what he knows. But first let's go back to the study. I want him faced with the body as he answers our questions."

They took him back out to the study. Remi winced as she saw Pier Paolo Manetti lying dead in a pool of his own vomit. The suspect winced as well.

Remi turned to him. "So you say you're a house guest. Tell me what happened."

"My name is Francesco Costa. I'm the most famous astrologer in Sicily." Remi stifled a chuckle. "We are working on a series for Italian television together. Pier Paolo was kind enough to let me stay at his house. I've been here for a couple of days. You can check the guest room upstairs and you will find my things. Call the station if you don't believe me. I know nothing of this!"

"Did you hear anything? See anyone?" Remi asked, unsure what to think of this strange little man. She hadn't had much experience with murderers in her career as a historian. That was beginning to change, though.

"No." Francesco gave a fearful look at the body. "I was out late last night and slept late. My village in Sicily is very small, so I don't often get to enjoy the pleasures of a big city. I didn't get back until four in the morning. I didn't hear Manetti, although I assumed he was asleep in the house. I went to the rooftop to observe the stars until dawn, and then I went to bed. Just as I was drifting off, I heard my host get up and go to the kitchen."

"What then?" Remi asked.

Francesco Costa shook his head. "Then I woke up, just half an hour ago. I went to the bathroom, took a shower, came downstairs, and found him. Not one minute later you came in."

Remi relayed all this to Daniel, who walked over to the body.

"I don't think he's been dead long. The vomit isn't dry, although it's not entirely liquid anymore either." He bent down and reached out. Remi's stomach did a backflip because she thought he was going to touch the vomit. Instead, he put a hand on Manetti's hand, and then the back of his neck. "Extremities are a bit cool, but the core body still retains a fair amount of warmth. He was killed quite recently. The hands might be cool because of poor circulation and lying here on the floor. I don't think he's been dead for more than an hour or so."

Remi turned to the suspect and pointed to the easel. "What was there?"

"A painting. It was covered. I didn't get to see it."

Remi frowned. Up until now she had been inclined to believe him. She suspected a lie now, though. Why wouldn't he show a guest his prize purchase? Unless he wanted to hide it, in which case he wouldn't have kept it in the living room.

"Manetti didn't show it to you? Didn't talk to you about it?"

"He didn't show it to me, but he planned to. He said it was a recent acquisition that he had cost him a great deal of money and trouble. He wanted my opinion on it but first wanted to know some more about astrology."

"More about astrology?"

"Yes, and not for the series. The planning for that was very basic. Astrology is a complex and ancient science, and for a television audience you are only explaining one-thousandth of the information. Manetti knew more than enough to do that himself. He didn't need my advice for the show's content; he needed me to help organize the material and act as a talking head."

"So what was he questioning you about?" Remi asked.

"Very specialized information. It's difficult to explain to a layperson."

"Explain it anyway," Remi said, slightly annoyed at the man's superior tone.

She glanced at Daniel, who was always impatient when she was speaking a language he didn't understand. He had decided to spend his time examining the room. She was surprised that he hadn't call the police yet, but considering how they had failed to protect Manetti, perhaps he wanted to examine the scene before they arrived.

"May I sit?" Francesco Costa pleaded. "This has all been too much for me."

"Go ahead," Remi said.

He moved to an armchair.

"Don't touch anything!" Daniel snapped at him. "This is a murder scene for Crissake!"

Francesco launched off the armchair as if pins were sticking out of the cushion.

"What did he say?" Francesco asked.

"He got mad at you touching the chair," Remi said, shooting an apologetic look at her frustrated partner. He had already gone back to investigating the room and didn't notice. "All right, Signor Costa, what did Manetti ask you about astrology?"

"He wanted to know about the use of astrological symbols in the early modern times, especially in the Low Countries in the 17th centuries. He asked about specific constellations and their symbolism."

"Such as?"

Francesco shrugged, the handcuffs around his wrists rattling.

"Everything. We talked for hours. I got a strange impression from it all. It was like he didn't want to ask what he was really interested in, so he asked about a wide range of subjects. At times he looked distracted, listening with only half an ear while thinking about other things. At other times he was on the edge of his seat."

"And when were those times?"

"When I spoke to him about the apocalyptic traditions in astrology, and how people in the past looked to the stars to determine the future, much like we do today."

Remi felt her skin prickle. That was it! The Second Coming, heralded by the Four Horsemen of the Apocalypse. She had begun to sense that might be the answer, and now she had confirmation.

Each of the paintings featured stars. Together those stars would indicate constellations at certain times of the year. That would create a horoscope, and that horoscope would predict the End Times.

The killer needed all four paintings in order to cast that horoscope.

And once he had that information, then what?

Another prickle of Remi's skin. What had Daniel said on the plane? Once someone became a serial killer, they didn't stop killing until they were stopped.

He doesn't just want to know the date of the End Times; he wants to be part of it.

Daniel's voice snapped her out of her thoughts.

"Look at this," he said from over at the bookshelf. "There's an entire library here of books on everything from Atlantis to reincarnation. What a nut. But the biggest and newest section is on astrology. See how many of these books are older editions that have been thumbed through over the years? No so much with the astrology books. Many are new, and I've found three so far where he was using the receipt as a bookmark. All bought in the last couple of months. Those paintings all had stars. You think he was trying to read something off the painting of Pestilence?"

Remi looked at her partner with new admiration.

We really do work well together, she thought. *I hope this gets to continue.*

She took a glance at poor Pier Paolo Manetti, still lying face down in a pool of vomit.

Maybe without so many corpses.

Turning back to Daniel, she said, "He needs all four paintings to cast a horoscope. Manetti brought in Sr. Costa here to learn more about the astrology of the period. I think the documentary was an excuse to hide his real motives."

Daniel's face fell. "Oh, damn. He's going to use that for the mother of all slaughters."

"Maybe the horoscope will say the End Times start a hundred years from now," Remi said, more hoping than believing.

Daniel shook his head. "That's not how these nutcases work. Either he'll read the horoscope to predict the Apocalypse starts next week, or he'll decide that even if the world is supposed to end in 2100, that he needs to set the groundwork by killing a bunch of people."

Remi's throat went dry. "We need to find that fourth painting. Now."

Daniel gave Francesco Costa a dismissive glance and turned back to Remi.

"To do that we need to up our game. He's been a step ahead of us the entire time. And if he gets the fourth painting before we do, a whole lot more people are going to die."

Remi nodded. "And that means I have a lot more work to do. And I know just where to do it."

CHAPTER TWENTY ONE

Sitting in the archives of Florence's Uffizi Gallery, Remi pored over the records of the four paintings once again, looking for any trace of evidence of the painting of Famine by Frerik Peeters. There was nothing. Her Dutch friend, the Belgian art curator Eleah Smets, had also double checked and come up with nothing.

Remi had hoped that the Uffizi, as one of Europe's great art museums, might have something new on the Four Horsemen of the Apocalypse, but once again she had come up short. She knew she had been grasping at straws. The Uffizi specialized in Italian art, not outré paintings by minor Dutch artists.

And certainly nothing about the set's most elusive painting. Other than a few references to Hendrick van Berckenrode commissioning the piece, there was no trace of the painting of Famine at all. It was like it had vanished into thin air.

Remi growled in frustration and leaned back from her chair, rubbing her temples.

"Nothing?" Daniel asked. He had been sitting nearby, talking to contacts on his mobile phone. He had also come up with nothing.

"No," Remi sighed. "What time is it?"

"Ten. We've been here for hours." He didn't say this out of any complaint, but merely frustration. The local police had gotten the Uffizi's curators to keep the archives open as long as Remi needed them. It was the least they could do to after bungling their monitoring of Manetti.

Further investigation of the house had revealed nothing of importance. No evidence had been found that Costa had any hand in the murder, nor had flight records shown he had been outside of Italy for more than a year.

Frustratingly, there were no notes on astrology or marks in any of Manetti's books on the subject. Nothing to help them understand better what he had been delving into. Whatever he had wanted to know about his painting, he had kept it in his head, and that knowledge had died with him.

So Remi had been stuck here in the archives looking for historical clues, instead of out on the streets looking for a serial murderer. All the while, she was bothered by the knowledge that the archives holding the answers to her questions about the Church of St. Pantaleon of Nicomedia were only a ten-minute taxi ride away. The next step, perhaps the last step, to her learning the secret of the cryptex, the medieval riddle that had intrigued her for her entire professional career.

"I don't know what to do," Remi said, gesturing with despair at the piles of old books and files in front of her. "No records, no bills of sale ..."

"What if it was never sold?" Daniel asked.

Remi looked up. "I beg your pardon?"

"You were saying that there's no record of the paintings ever having been together. Maybe that was part of the plan. They held this great secret, so you couldn't have them all hanging in the same room or someone who knew astrology might figure it out. So they were kept in separate houses or separate cities. Maybe even separate countries, even right at the beginning. What if Hendrick van Berckenrode allowed Frerik Peeters to keep his painting of Famine, wanting one to stay close while the other three got sold elsewhere? Then maybe it never got sold after that. It might have stayed in the family all this time. My mother took me to aristocratic houses here in Europe where there have been paintings kept by the family for centuries."

Remi's jaw dropped. "I ... I never thought of that. You might be right. That's brilliant!"

And I'm a fool. Why didn't I think of that? It's my job to think of these things.

Remi pulled out her phone.

"What are you doing?" Daniel asked.

"It's still afternoon in the United States. I'm texting a genealogist I know to look up any surviving relatives of Frerik Peeters."

"After four hundred years? Aren't there going to be heaps of them?"

"Yes, but we'll look for direct descendants, not nephews or nieces. If we're lucky, we'll find Peeters's great-great-grandson."

"Add a few greats to that. This is a hell of a long shot."

Remi looked at him sadly. "Long shots are all we have now."

* * *

Remi's genealogist colleague pulled an all-nighter in the United States to trace the complex history and lineage of the Peeters family, which meant that it wasn't until Remi had spent a restless night at the hotel and a nervous morning constantly checking her phone before she finally got an answer back.

When she did, all was forgiven. The genealogist had struck gold.

Italo Peeters, the many-times-great-grandson of Frerik Peeters, lived in Bologna, just an hour and a half drive from Florence. The son of a Dutch father and Italian mother, he had worked as an accountant before his retirement the year before.

Torsson found he had a criminal record. His ex-wife lodged a complaint of physical abuse and used it as ground for divorce. Peeters had also been in trouble with the law for drunk and disorderly conduct, damage to property when a café tried to kick him out and he went on a rampage. He had also paid a hefty fine for defecating on a peace memorial.

"Sounds like a charmer," Daniel said when the Interpol agent read out the list to them.

"There's more," Torsson said. "Phone records show he had called Manetti several times in the past few weeks."

"Did Manetti call him?" Remi asked.

"No. Odd, isn't it?"

"Perhaps not," Remi mused. "Maybe he heard somehow that Manetti had purchased Pestilence. Then he tracked down his phone number and started badgering him to sell it."

"And when that didn't work, he decided to take what he wanted?" Danicl said. "Ycah, could be."

"The only problem with that theory is there are no flight records showing him going to the United States," Torsson said. "He could have gone to France on the train, paying cash, but there would be a record if he boarded an international flight."

"The killer has shown himself to be very resourceful," Remi said. "Perhaps he has a false passport."

"Those aren't too hard to buy here in Europe," Torsson conceded. "Especially Belgian passports. There was a big scandal a few years ago when it was discovered Belgian officials had sold thousands of blank passports to the black market."

"Ah, Europe. So civilized," Daniel said. That got him sour looks from the two Europeans.

Remi decided to ignore the comment. "We need to get to Bologna."

Daniel nodded. "Even if the Belgians didn't help him out, there's always the possibility that he hired someone to make the U.S. hit. And if he isn't the perpetrator, he might be the next victim. Torsson, call ahead to the Bologna police to put him in protective custody. And make sure they do a better job than the idiots here in Florence."

Torsson got on the phone. "I'll also ask them if he has a painting of Famine in his house. Then I'll rent a car for us."

* * *

Within an hour they were on the highway out of Florence in a rented car with the Interpol agent at the wheel, weaving through traffic and breaking the speed limit with all the enthusiasm of someone who knew the law was on his side.

His phone rang.

"Try not to kill us when you answer that," Remi said from the back seat.

He chuckled, pulled out his phone and answered it in English. "Hello? You can't? *Parlez-vous francais? Non?* One moment."

He handed the phone back to Remi. "The arresting officer's English isn't up to the task, and my Italian isn't much better. You speak with him."

Remi took the phone. "Hello, this is Remi Laurent speaking, civilian advisor to the Federal Bureau of Investigation."

"Hello," a gruff male voice said. "This is Aurelio Russo of the Bologna police department. Is agent Daniel Walker there?"

"I'm afraid he doesn't speak Italian." *Or at least doesn't admit to.*

"Is there no other officer of the law there I can speak to?"

Remi frowned. *You mean a man?* He had used the masculine form of the word in Italian. "I'm the only one in the car who speaks Italian, and I am temporarily an officer of the law."

Remi shot a nervous glance at Daniel, but her partner didn't react.

At least he didn't understand that *bit of Italian.*

"Very well," Officer Russo said, sounding irritated. "We found the painting you requested."

Remi's heart took a few skips.

“Where was it?”

“Hanging in his dining room.”

Remi cocked her head. Who would keep a painting of Famine in their dining room?

A psychotic, that’s who.

“Keep him in custody. We’ll be there as soon as we can.”

“Are those Agent Walker’s orders?”

“Yes,” Remi snapped, hanging up.

She wished she could have slammed it. That was the only thing she missed about the old landline phones. You could give them a good slam when you felt like it.

But she couldn’t stay angry for long. They were finally about to see one of the Four Horsemen of the Apocalypse face to face.

CHAPTER TWENTY TWO

Daniel felt a tug of disappointment when they arrived at the house of Italo Peeters. He had expected some grandiose old palace in the center of town like Pier Paolo Manetti's home, or some luxurious mansion like that of Montgomery Dyson, or some fine art studio like Pierre Lafontaine's place.

Instead, he found himself entering a humdrum apartment on the edge of town, spacious but modern and utterly unremarkable.

At least until he got inside.

Once past the local police officer guarding the door, he came to a living room that was anything but unremarkable. The walls were covered in paintings and framed sketches on old parchment and vellum. The art all looked like it dated to the 17th century, and included three small religious paintings, several complex alchemical engravings full of symbolism Daniel didn't understand, and a series of sketches showing soldiers killing children.

In one, a soldier held a naked infant up high while slashing down on another small child with his sword.

Daniel's stomach clenched.

He shot a warning look to Remi and Torsson that told them he wanted to question the suspect himself, then turned angrily to the nondescript man who sat in an armchair in one corner. Compared with the art, the man was so unremarkable that it was easy to forget he was there.

"Are you Italo Peeters? Do you speak English?"

"Yes, and I do speak English," he said with not too much of an accent. "I was told agents from the FBI and Interpol were coming to speak to me. What's this all about?"

The confusion in his voice sounded genuine, at odds with the gruesome art on his walls. Daniel studied him. He wore a tan sweater over a pink dress shirt, brown slacks, and dress shoes. His receding gray hair and neatly trimmed beard framed wire-rimmed spectacles. He sure looked like an accountant.

And the room, minus the art, looked like an accountant's apartment—subdued carpeting, conservative furniture, a small bookshelf with nothing but popular novels, and a big TV and high-end stereo system.

"I heard you have in your possession the painting of Famine by Frerik Peeters."

"That's right. He was my ancestor. That painting and these other works," he gestured at the walls, "are all by him."

Daniel made a significant look around the room. "Interesting subject matter."

Italo Peeters's face transformed. The confusion and concern regarding his situation vanished, replaced with a bright-eyed enthusiasm. The change was as sudden as it was shocking.

"Wonderful, aren't they?" he said, leaning forward. "My ancestor was a genius. He showed the world as it really was."

Daniel resisted the urge to say something nasty and looked around the room again. Peeters was in custody, and before Daniel made an arrest, assuming he found grounds for an arrest, he wanted to get into the man's mind.

The alchemical engravings all showed the interiors of laboratories with various beakers, kettles, and instruments Daniel couldn't identify being used by hunched old men in search of … something. Various symbols such as crescent moons, three-faced naked women, and crossed swords hung over the scenes. In the corners, little demons pointed and laughed at the alchemist, or hid behind the alembics and retorts, secretly assisting his labor. Punishment for the sin of alchemy or assisting a willing man down the path of evil?

The religious paintings were fewer and showed various saints suffering the pains of martyrdom. Saint Sebastian writhed against a tree as archers pincushioned him with arrows, the blood streaming from a dozen wounds painting in loving detail. A naked Saint Lawrence lay on a grill, the flames beneath heating the iron red hot, his flesh searing off his bones. An equally naked St. Catherine was shown being broken on the wheel. The woman, eyes raised to heaven, was tied spread-eagled onto a wagon wheel on the ground as a trio of Roman legionaries bludgeoned her with clubs in order to break her bones. Her limbs were all twisted at unnatural angles, the jagged ends of the broken bones sticking through bloody wounds.

Daniel recalled that St. Catherine hadn't actually been broken on the wheel. The Romans had intended to kill her that way, but the wheel miraculously shattered, proving she was protected by the grace of God. Frerik Peeters hadn't been able to resist showing her getting tortured in this gruesome manner. If he had displayed this image publicly back then, he would have probably gotten in trouble with Church authorities for calling into doubt the saint's holiness.

Given Italo Peeters's history of spouse abuse, Daniel bet this was his favorite image.

The most numerous works of "art" were the sketches of soldiers slaughtering children, often in front of their pleading or dying parents. The detail and variety of the atrocities was too much for Daniel to look at, even in a sketch.

He turned back to Peeters. "So which are your favorites?"

The suspect, seeming to forget the fact that he was in the presence of several police officers, said eagerly, "Oh, definitely the studies for the St. Bartholomew's Day Massacre. What works of art! Are you familiar with the event? It was during the Wars of Religion between Catholics and Protestants. A Catholic mob tried to exterminate every Huguenot in Paris. Some say the mob exterminated up to 30,000 Protestants. Men, women, children. Even babies. While I am not religious myself, at least not in the traditional sense, you have to admire their zeal. They would do anything, absolutely anything, in order to support their cause."

Daniel heard a sharp intake of breath from Remi. Briefly he wondered what the art historian thought of these "works of art."

He sure knew what he thought of them.

Before he could share with Peeters, the suspect raised a finger. "But the best, the absolute best, is in my dining room. May I show you?"

"Be my guest," Daniel said, his sarcasm seemingly lost on this nutcase.

Thank God I'm carrying a gun. I have to make sure he doesn't go anywhere near the kitchen. If he so much as looks at a knife, I'm plugging him.

Peeters said something to the Italian police officer standing by him and rose from his armchair. The officer walked ahead, while Daniel walked just behind the suspect, ready to subdue him if he tried to make a move. Torsson and Remi took up the rear.

They entered a small dining room with an old oak table, a sideboard with some china, and a single painting on the wall.

Remi took in another breath. Daniel did too.

For that painting was Famine by Frerik Peeters.

It was the first of the paintings they had seen outside a grainy old photograph, and they hadn't seen any image at all of this one.

Even though Daniel already knew the dimensions of the four panels, he was still surprised at how small it was—only about four feet tall and less than three feet wide. The four panels hung together would only adorn one wall of a mid-sized room.

What Frerik Peeters had sacrificed in size he made up for in subject matter. An emaciated man rode a black horse, holding up a pair of brass scales in his claw-like hand. The horse was trampling a crowd of starving people beneath its hooves, their skeletally thin bodies lying so close together as to make a bony carpet. Above, a brilliant spread of stars shone in the night sky.

"This is his masterpiece," Peeters enthused. "Kept in my family for four hundred years. It was commissioned by Hendrick van Berckenrode, the mayor of Haarlem in its golden age. It was originally one of a set, each piece showing one of the Four Horsemen of the Apocalypse. It has long been my dream to reunite the set. They were done by different artists and have been scattered over the years. I suspect this is the best. Just look at the detail! The artistry! Look at the faces of the dying, how, despite their exhaustion, they are contorted by terror at seeing death approach. And look at the starshine on the brass scales. Beautiful. Scales such as these were used by the authorities to measure out rations of grain in times of famine. But as you can see, there is no grain on them. No food for these people. Ha ha!"

Peeters covered his mouth and cleared his throat.

"I am sorry, but I got carried away, as I always do when I speak of my brilliant ancestor. Why are you here? Has some work of Frerik's been stolen and you need me as a civilian consultant?"

This time Daniel did look at Remi, who had an unreasonable expression masking her emotions. She was probably thinking the same thing he was—is this guy really that clueless or is he playing a game with them?

Well, if he's playing a game, he's going to lose.

Daniel turned back to Italo Peeters. "You mentioned you'd like to reunite the set. Have you ever tried to do that?"

"Yes," he said with surprising candor. "I've done a great deal of research on my ancestor, and of course that included his collaborations with other artists of the period. I had a lot of trouble tracking them down. Luckily through a rare book dealer I found an old exhibition catalog from Amsterdam where Pestilence and War were for sale, but there was no record of who they sold to, and I could never trace them."

Daniel studied him for a moment. That sounded like the same catalog Remi had come upon in an archive in New York. So he was telling a bit of the truth.

But was he telling all of it?

Remembering his criminal history, Daniel decided to probe him. He put on a sarcastic smile and said,

"Kind of strange having a painting of Famine in the dining room, don't you think? What does your wife think of that?"

Peeters's face darkened and a dangerous glint came to his eyes. His hands balled into fists and a low growl rose from his throat. The transformation was so sudden and so complete that Daniel almost went for his gun. The Italian police officer stepped up behind the suspect, arms slightly apart.

"That BITCH didn't appreciate art! I couldn't have any of my ancestor's paintings up when she still lived here. I had to keep Famine tucked away in a closet, and the smaller works in a folder that I could only look at when she wasn't around. Augh! No appreciation for beauty. Marrying her was the biggest mistake of my life."

"So you slapped her around," Daniel said, anger rising in him.

"I tried to slap some sense into her, as you Americans say. Bah! I should have known it wouldn't do any good. She was Italian, and Italians have been weak for centuries. Look at their art! All bright colors and pudgy ladies and little angels. They didn't paint anything *real*. Now in my country they had true art. It showed how things really were. Not a bunch of fluffy clouds and some pansy Jesus floating above them, but martyrs suffering the most exquisite tortures. I can't stand this country."

"I thought you were Italian."

"I've lived here all my life," he said like he was saying something dirty. "My father is Dutch, but my mother was Italian. My mother named me Italo to emphasize my Italian side. But make no mistake. I'm one hundred percent Dutch."

"So where is your wife now?"

"The BITCH is out of my life, thank God and good riddance."

"So now you can sit in your apartment looking at famine and exquisite tortures," Daniel said, mimicking his words.

Peeters gave him a smug smile.

Interesting choice of words he used. "Exquisite". That's not a negative word, and his English is good enough he knows what he's saying. He loves these paintings.

Damn, he's as sick as his ancestor.

But am I facing the murderer?

Daniel still wasn't sure. Ninety percent, but not a hundred.

"You mentioned you've searched for the rest of the Four Horsemen. Have you been looking recently?"

Peeters shook his head. "No. I haven't been out of the country in almost a year. The last time was to Greece with the BITCH. Our last wasted vacation together. Sadly, I've given up trying to find the paintings. Every time I think I've found out something, I find myself at a dead end."

Tell me about it.

But it's interesting that you emphasized you haven't been out of the country. I didn't ask that. And when a suspect answers a question I haven't asked, it's because it's the question he's afraid of answering truthfully.

And Torsson said he could take a train to Paris using cash without any record. Thanks to the European Union, there isn't a hard border between Italy and France anymore.

The Interpol agent touched his elbow and nodded toward the door.

Daniel followed him. On his way out the room, he said to Remi, who was standing on the other side of the table from Peeters, "If you have any questions, feel free to ask him."

Peeters sneered. "I don't speak with that kind of creature."

Remi looked like she wanted to pull out her pepper spray and give him a dose. Daniel kind of hoped she would.

"On that note," Daniel grumbled, "I need to speak with my colleague. Stay here and admire your painting."

"He won't admire it long," Torsson whispered to him. "What I discovered changes everything."

CHAPTER TWENTY THREE

Torsson led Daniel back to the living room. Stopping by a sketch of a file of soldiers marching with their spears sloped over their shoulders, each with a baby skewered on top, the Interpol agent told him,

"The Italian police fast tracked a search of his phone records. That story he gave about not being outside the country is untrue. He was in France just three months ago. Paris, as a matter of fact. He used his phone from Paris."

"Three months ago? That was before Lafontaine acquired the painting of War."

"Yes, but Lafontaine had been looking for it. And his assistant had said that he had become very secretive and worried about others looking for it."

Daniel grunted. "That's right. Maybe Lafontaine met Peeters and got a bad impression of him. He's a real charmer, as you saw. Lafontaine, with his art connections, got a hold of War and Peeters didn't. Maybe Peeters heard about it and didn't like it too much."

Torsson glanced in the direction of the dining room. "He does have a history of violence."

"But would he commit murder? Maybe. He certainly has sick fantasies. What about the phone records for when the murders were happening?"

"All show him in Bologna."

Daniel shrugged. "His phone was in Bologna. Any criminal with half a brain leaves his phone at home before going out to commit a crime."

"We've searched the house and his office and haven't found the other paintings."

"Once again, an intelligent criminal would stash them somewhere safer than that. This guy isn't exactly a model citizen, but he seems fairly intelligent given his job and level of education."

"You think we have our man?"

Daniel shook his head. "I think so, especially after that lie about France. I sure as hell am going to arrest him. We have enough circumstantial evidence to hold him for a day or two. If he's the killer, and I'm 99 percent sure he is, we can find evidence soon enough. If he isn't, then we need to keep him in protective custody."

Daniel and Torsson went back into the dining room, where Peeters stood gazing at the painting of his ancestor.

"Why didn't you tell me about your little trip to Paris three months ago?" Daniel asked in a curt tone.

Peeter's head whipped around, eyes wide. He recovered quickly, putting on a calm poise. "Oh, I forgot. A brief trip to see the Goya exhibition at the Louvre. Wonderful painter, Goya. Especially the paintings of the Napoleonic Wars. He could really see."

"What else did you do there?"

Peeters shrugged. "Nothing much."

"Did you search for the painting of War?"

Peeters's features hardened. "Agent Walker, I think that's enough questioning for now. If you wish to speak to me further, you'll have to speak with my attorney."

Daniel's eyes narrowed, his hand straying closer to the gun in his shoulder holster. This man was dangerous. Smart too, which made him even more dangerous.

"Mr. Peeters, it's in your best interest to cooperate with us."

The accountant looked him in the eye. "And I will. Through my lawyer."

Have it your way, dumbass. You can't bully me like you bullied your wife.

Daniel turned to Torsson. "You're Interpol, so you can make the arrest."

Peeters frowned. "On what charges?"

Torsson moved to Peeters's side. "For three counts of murder."

Peeters looked confused. "Murder?"

Daniel studied him closely as he said, "For the owners of the other Four Horsemen of the Apocalypse."

Peeters's eyes widened. A smile tugged at the edges of his mouth, taking Daniel aback. Peeters hung his head and tried to look serious. "I didn't do that."

Suspicion welled up in Daniel's heart.

Yeah, this guy is definitely up to something. That surprise looked genuine, though. Weird. Maybe he's not fully aware of his actions?

"Know who did?" Daniel asked.

"Talk to my lawyer."

Torsson led him out. Daniel watched him go, still not sure if they had captured a calculating killer or a sad, lonely man who had gone criminally insane.

* * *

Remi followed Torsson and the Italian officer as they led Italo Peeters outside, hurrying to catch up to them.

"Has anyone ever tried to steal your painting?" she asked.

Peeters looked annoyed and confused. "No. Hardly anyone knows I have it. Now go away, woman."

He said "woman" like it was an insult. Remi ignored the slight. This was too important.

"Has anyone ever threatened your life?"

"Besides my wife sucking the life out of me for the last twenty years? No. I don't know what your partner is talking about. Murders? Do I look like a murderer to you, you stupid woman? Now go away. I have nothing more to say."

The Italian officer opened the back of a police car parked at the curb and helped Peeters inside. He didn't look at her. This might be her last chance to get information. If he wasn't the murderer, he might have some knowledge that would help find who really was doing the killings.

He wouldn't do it out of any feelings for the greater good, since he obviously didn't have any, but he might do it out of self-preservation.

"Mr. Peeters, please. Someone is killing off the owners of the Four Horsemen one by one and stealing the paintings. I can tell you didn't do it." She hoped he believed that more than she did. "The killer already has three of the paintings. He's coming for you next. If you don't help us, he might get you."

Peeters snorted. "In a police station? Quiet, you cow."

"If he can't get you, he could get your painting."

"Take it to the police station, then. If it gets stolen, I'll sue!"

Protecting it made sense. "I'll take care of it, Mr. Peeters."

He glowered at her. "You?"

"I'm an art historian and I've worked as a curator at—"

"You won't touch my painting! Get a real curator to handle it."

The officer slammed the door shut on him.

You mean a male curator? Right because "real" art curators don't have breasts, even though the majority of them do.

Idiot. I'm tempted to leave you to the killer.

Or are you the killer? You certainly have plenty of hate boiling inside you. And a fair bit of madness too.

The police officer and Torsson got in the patrol car and drove off, leaving Remi to stand on the sidewalk, wondering.

An impulse made her pull out her phone and check her messages. No calls or texts from Cyril. She checked her email and her heart leapt. An email from him!

A moment later, she slumped. It was only a message about a meeting, sent to the entire history faculty because he was department head. It wasn't specifically to her.

Had he included her in the message as a deliberate snub, knowing she wouldn't be there to attend but wanting to show that life went on without her, that he could send a work email without sending a personal one addressing their fight?

Or had it slipped his mind entirely? Had he just sent that routine message out to the faculty without a thought of her at all?

Both possibilities sent a wave of depression over her.

She looked around the quiet street. A café stood across the way, nearly full as people enjoyed a coffee in the sunshine. A clothing store and a small supermarket stood next to it. The rest of the street was lined with modern apartment buildings much like the one where Italo Peeters lived. People moved up and down the street doing their shopping or going to or from home, totally unaware that in this mundane neighborhood a man had just been arrested on suspicion of murder and a woman was feeling her heart break.

* * *

The Fifth Horseman watched from the café across the street as Italo Peeters was led to the police car. He cursed his luck and he cursed himself. After poisoning Pier Paolo Manetti and taking the portrait of Pestilence, he had allowed himself a brief rest. Just a couple of hours to take a nap and to admire the three paintings he already had.

The set had almost been complete, and already the pattern of stars was hinting at the final answer. That had dazzled him for a time when he really should have been driving as fast as he could to Bologna to kill Peeters and get the final painting.

Foolish. A moment's weakness and the answer, almost within his grasp, had been snatched from him.

Rage seethed in him as the police car drove away, taking his fourth victim out of reach.

No, he couldn't fail now. Not after so many years of painstaking research. Not after so many years of sacrifice. He had to get the painting of Famine. He had to kill Peeters in the appropriate manner.

Both tasks had to be accomplished. The fourth painting was essential to understand the whole. That's why they had always been kept separate. And each owner had to be punished for their folly in their own special way.

For only he, the Fifth Horseman, could understand the key. They all thought they could unlock it, and perhaps given enough time they could have. Montgomery Dyson had the resources. Pierre Lafontaine had the background. Pier Paolo Manetti had the connections. Italo Peeters had the spirit.

But only he had the wisdom.

And only he had the cunning.

Such as now. An Italian woman in her forties was standing uncertainly at the edge of the café, looking for an empty table. There was none. He waved over to her with the guidebook he used as a prop and said with his distinctive American accent.

"Ma'am, if you don't mind sharing a table, you can sit over here."

The woman looked at him, hesitating. He gave her the innocent, open smile of a tourist. She smiled back and sat.

"Thank you," she said.

"No problem. I love your city. So beautiful, and great food."

"Oh, I'm happy you're having a good vacation. Have you been in Italy long?"

"Not too long. I'll be here a little while yet."

With that, he opened his guidebook and pretended to read. The woman, having shared enough conversation for courtesy's sake, pulled out her phone.

The Fifth Horseman suppressed a smile. Good. The police were looking for a lone man. They would never suspect a couple, which is what they now looked like to the casual eye.

Now he could sit here for a while without fear and see what the police did. Italy's famously slow service would ensure the woman would be here for at least half an hour.

Yes. He would watch, and he would wait. No one, not even the police, could stop him now.

CHAPTER TWENTY FOUR

Daniel watched as a curator from a local museum wrapped up the painting of Famine. A policeman stood nearby, as did Remi.

She looked seriously pissed.

"I could have done this," she grumbled for the hundredth time. "I've been working with fine art my entire professional career."

"If Peeters turns out to be innocent, the cops don't want a lawsuit on their hands," Daniel replied, also for the hundredth time.

Remi muttered something in French, then switched to English for his benefit. "He wanted a man to do the job."

"Serial killers aren't generally known for their staunch support of feminism."

"Very funny." She looked at him curiously. "Do you really think it's him?"

Daniel scratched his jaw, noticing he needed a shave. "I don't know. He fits. He lied about going to France and the moment we challenged him on it he lawyered up. He also has a history of violence. And yet … "

"Your gut says it isn't him."

"My gut isn't sure. But my gut has been wrong before."

"How often?"

Daniel smiled. "Not often."

"My gut isn't sure," Remi admitted.

"Your gut needs more experience. You've been getting plenty lately."

Remi grimaced. "Perhaps too much."

Daniel laughed. "Oh, come on. You love it!"

Remi shot him a sly smile. Then her stomach grumbled.

"Sounds like your gut's got other concerns," Daniel said.

"When was the last time we ate?" she asked.

Daniel shrugged. "Not sure. That happens on this job. You'll get used to it. Torsson said the Italian police take their time processing prisoners. We won't get to question Peeters again for another couple of hours. Let's go get something to eat."

Remi gave the painting a nervous glance. The curator had finished wrapping it up and lifted it off the dining room table.

"Are you sure the painting will be safe?" she asked.

"It's going in a police car to the police station," Daniel said patiently. "Yes, it will be safe. Don't worry."

"I'm not going to stop worrying until we have our man or are sure Peeters is the culprit."

"Neither will I," Daniel admitted. "But still, the painting will be safe at the station."

Remi turned to the curator, and they spoke in Italian for a moment; then the curator and the local police officer headed for the door. Daniel and Remi followed. Two local detectives sat in the living room. They gave them a nod as they left. The pair would stay in the apartment round the clock, in case the murderer made an appearance.

The curator carried the painting down the steps to the curb, Remi fretting just behind and issuing what sounded like instructions to the poor man. He just nodded and kept doing what he was doing.

Once they got to the police car parked out front, Daniel scanned the area. Across the street, the café was full. He saw no single men sitting there. A few couples, sure, but this guy struck Daniel as an obsessive, and most obsessive were loners. Daniel didn't see any lone men on the street either, except for a guy walking his dog who was at least a foot too short to be the perp.

Wait, who was that? Leaning against a telephone pole half a block down the street was a muscular man in his forties reading a newspaper.

Or at least pretending to read a newspaper. He kept looking around, and not being too subtle about it either.

Thc curator put thc painting in thc back scat of thc policc car as Remi fussed with him in Italian. The cop stood idly by.

Daniel kept an eye on the guy with the newspaper. For a moment the man looked at his newspaper, then right at Daniel and his companions.

Daniel's hand strayed toward the inside of his jacket, where he had his shoulder holster.

The man looked away, scanning the street. Looking for more police?

Just then his face lit up, he folded the newspaper, and opened his arms wide.

A woman in her thirties, leading a small boy by the hand, crossed the street near him. The boy squealed with delight, ran up to the man, who lifted him high in the air. The woman gave him a kiss and the three of them walked away, the newspaper man giving the boy a piggyback ride.

So much for that suspect.

Daniel looked around again and saw no other lone men. A lot of the people in the café and on the street were watching them, of course. A police car always attracts attention. It was nothing unusual.

The policeman closed the back door to his patrol car and the curator said goodbye. The cop said something in Italian to Remi.

"What's that?" Daniel asked.

"He says Peeters is getting processed and won't be available for questioning for at least another hour."

"Torsson said two hours."

"Torsson was being realistic."

Daniel grinned. "Well, since we got a spare moment, let's get some lunch. The detectives here can cover Peeters's apartment. One of them speaks English and told me he'd call if they saw anything suspicious."

"All right. I could use something to eat. And a coffee."

"Especially a coffee," Daniel groaned, the stress and grind of the previous few days suddenly feeling like a heavy weight on his entire body. And Remi looked the way he felt.

"The police station is downtown. How about we go with him there and then find a good place?" Remi suggested.

Daniel smiled. "You just don't want that painting out of your sight, do you?"

Remi smiled back. "Guilty as charged."

They got in the car, Remi sitting in back and holding the painting as the officer drove through the narrow streets to the station. Daniel looked out the window. Bologna wasn't as ornate as Florence, but it still had its old stone palaces with crests over the heavy wooden doors, its Renaissance churches so modest on the outside and glorious with stained glass and gold altars on the inside, and its fountains on the corners with marble dolphins spouting out water.

Also, unlike Florence, it was not entirely overrun with tourists. Sure, there were crowds, but not the hordes he had seen on this current visit and the one he had made here when he was thirteen.

Bologna had a third and most important difference. In his teenaged travels through Italy with Mom and the Monster, as he sometimes called them, they never stopped in Bologna. He could look out and appreciate the scene without it being soured by old memories.

They stopped at the police station and Remi insisted on carrying in the painting herself, not letting it go until it was safely stored in an evidence locker, the officer on duty being given strict instructions not to touch it in her absence. The man kept a poker face, and Daniel wondered if he was taking her seriously.

Torsson appeared as they were leaving the station.

"They told me you were here," the Swede said.

"Yeah, we're going to get some lunch," Daniel said.

"Enjoy. I need to stay here and do some paperwork. One of the detectives is ordering some pasta to be delivered. As I expected, Peeters is in a holding cell, waiting to be processed."

"All right," Daniel said. "We'll see you in about an hour."

As they stepped out of the station, Daniel wondered at the relief he felt that Torsson was staying behind. He'd proved to be a good cop and a decent travel companion so why would he not want him to come along?

"Let's go this way," Remi said, pointing to a narrow lane. "I have something to show you."

"A free tour guide to Bologna! I'm in luck." Daniel's mood brightened.

"Not free. You can buy me lunch," she said with a smile.

"The FBI will buy you lunch. Take everything you can from those bureaucratic bean counters."

"Fair cnough. Wc don't havc much timc, but I'd likc to show you Bologna's great attraction. Then we can get a bite to eat. It's not far."

Remi must have planned the street she had taken him down for maximum effect, because as they turned a corner, Daniel stopped and gaped.

Two square stone towers, about three hundred feet tall, stood before them. He had noticed a couple of smaller towers around town; they were a common sight in Italy, but he had never seen any so massive. Their sides were pierced with arrow slits, the top of one crenelated. It looked like a playful giant had grabbed the tops of a pair of castles and stretched them all out of proportion. The taller one had a distinct tilt.

Not as marked as the Leaning Tower of Pisa, but enough to make Daniel wonder what would happen to it in a few years.

"These are the towers of Asinelli and Garisenda," Remi said. "Those were the families that built them in the 12th century. It was common for important families in the Italian city-states to build towers for defense. And also to show off."

"If they wanted to impress me, they've succeeded."

"They've succeeded with everyone who has come here in the last eight hundred years. Perhaps we can find a space in a café in sight of one of them."

Daniel looked up at the taller tower for a moment.

"How about we climb to the top?" he said quietly.

"You have the energy for that? I feel like taking a week-long nap."

"So do I. Let's do it anyway."

Remi stared at him a moment, then shrugged. "All right."

Daniel and Remi walked to the base of the tower. The two towers were at an intersection of five roads in a big plaza lined with shops and cafés.

"Are you sure you want to climb all the way to the top?" Remi asked. "There's no elevator."

"I'm aware that there were no elevators in the 12th century."

A ticket agent was posted just inside the tower's stone portal. Daniel paid for both of them, and they entered.

Once inside, they came to a staircase running around the inside of the tower. Daniel looked up …

… and up.

"Whoa," he said.

"Are you afraid of heights?" Remi asked.

"I'm not afraid of anything except anchovies on pizza. Let's go."

They started up the stairs, Daniel taking the lead. The wooden stairs took them around and around, the top of the tower far overhead, the ground floor gradually dwindling beneath their feet. Every now and then he ran his hand along the smooth, cool stones, imagining the centuries of soldiers and noblemen who had climbed these stairs before him.

What had their lives been like? Had they enjoyed the kind of sick paintings he and Remi were tracking down, or had they been decent citizens? Maybe some of them had been on the city watch, chasing down criminals.

Daniel smiled at the thought. Maybe he was walking in the footsteps of some medieval Daniel Walker. A brilliant investigator tracking down poisoners and plotters in the streets of Bologna's golden age.

So what would the medieval Daniel Walker think of this case? Would he be able to look Peeters in the eye and see if he was guilty of innocent? Back then, he could have put the guy on the rack and found out the truth soon enough. The modern Daniel Walker was stuck with interrogation while the defendant was shielded by a lawyer.

This was just a brief respite, a bit of tourism while Peeters was getting processed. It would be back to work soon enough. Back to the fight against evil. He wondered if his medieval counterpart would have faced more, or less, evil in his time. Probably the same. Human nature didn't change all that much.

The medieval Daniel Walker would have probably been better at these steps, though. The modern one was already getting out of breath. Sweat trickled down his back and he flapped his jacket, which felt stuffy. His shoulder holster felt heavier and heavier.

He kept climbing. He didn't want to embarrass himself in front of Remi and besides, he wanted to get to the top.

Still, he found himself slowing, his breath coming faster.

Damn. Maybe I should start going to the gym like everyone says.

"Are you all right?" Remi asked.

"Sure, why do you ask?"

His effort at nonchalance came out as a strangled gasp.

"We can slow down if you want to."

"No sweat."

Daniel looked up. Big mistake. The top was still far, far above. Maybe this was a bad idea.

Man up, he told himself. *Let's see a bit of Italy with some good company for a change.*

He started climbing faster, ignoring the pounding in his chest and the lead in his feet.

You never thought you'd come back to Europe, and now here you are. See some of it. For real, this time.

After what seemed like ages, they finally emerged on top. A stiff breeze cooled him, and the sun shone merrily on an open platform surrounded by a crenellated wall. A few other tourists stood snapping photos. Daniel went to the edge and looked over.

All of Bologna lay spread below him. Far, far below, tiny cars and people passed through the square, its five streets running out in all directions like the spokes of a wheel to the gates of the old city wall. Red roofed buildings, large gabled churches, and a few other, shorter towers could be seen in all directions. In the distance rose green hills dotted with farmhouses.

"Is the view worth the climb?" Remi asked. Daniel was secretly happy to hear she was out of breath too.

Daniel only nodded.

He made a slow circuit of the top of the tower, taking in the stunning view.

"This apparently was the tallest of the towers ever built," Remi said. "There were more than a hundred in Bologna in its glory days. Now there's only twenty-one."

"This is enough," Daniel said, staring.

This is the kind of place he liked. Isolated. He would have had us climb up here right at opening time or just as people were clearing out at closing. He would have gotten me alone up here. It would have been a risk, but he liked the risk.

Daniel shook his head to clear the ugly thoughts.

He didn't take you here. This is yours.

"You like it?" Remi asked.

"Yeah," Daniel said, nodding. "Yeah, I do."

He sucked in a deep breath and turned to Remi.

"Let's go. We have work to do. I'm sure you took photos of Famine, and you have those photos of the other paintings. Let's see if we can figure out what those paintings mean as a set."

"You don't want to stay a little longer?"

"I've seen what I needed to see," he said. "Thank you."

CHAPTER TWENTY FIVE

Remi soon discovered that astrology wasn't her specialty. They sat at a café in sight of the two towers—Daniel had insisted on that—eating Tagliatelle alla Bolognese and staring at the pictures on her phone.

She had images of all four paintings now, those taken on her own phone of Famine and grainy black and white ones of Death, Pestilence, and War from old publications. While the quality of three out of four of the photos was far from ideal, they showed enough that she could figure out the patterns of stars. After much back on forth on their phones, looking at constellations on an astrology site and then back at the photos, Remi and Daniel could make an educated guess of what constellations the paintings showed.

Not that it told her anything. Famine showed the constellation of Pisces, which Remi interpreted as a wry joke about fasting. People were not supposed to eat meat on fasting days, which in the olden days included Fridays since that was the day Jesus died. Fish, being cold-blooded, were exempt from this rule. Of course, the people in the painting of Famine were on a far more stringent fast, and to gaze up at the oversized constellation of Pisces right above Famine's empty scales was a bit of cruel humor.

Squinting hard at the tavern sign on the painting of Pestilence, she thought she recognized the constellation of Lyra, the harp. One of the people dying of disease also had a harp, so that made her a bit more sure, but not a hundred percent.

For War and Death, the images weren't as clear.

War, as much as they could see from the old photo, was set in the daytime. But there was that figure of the scholar Remi had noticed before, the only person not looking at the armored figure coming to cut everyone down. Instead, he looked at a book that looked like it showed a pattern of stars. One star shone much brighter than the others.

"What could that be?" Remi asked. "I don't know of a constellation that has one star so much brighter than the rest."

"Maybe it's a planet," Daniel suggested.

"Mars!" they both said together, making a young woman glance over from the next table.

"The god of war passing through some constellation," Remi said in a lower voice. "That would signal war. I think the constellation is Sagittarius. That's a centaur, but also an archer. It makes sense as a constellation of war."

"None of this makes sense," Daniel grumbled.

"Not yet. We have to keep trying. Let's look at Death."

The young woman's eyes widened. Remi shot her a smile and she hurriedly went back to her coffee.

The grainy, secondhand black and white photo of Death was somewhat clearer. Death's scythe framed the constellation of Orion. The Hunter. That seemed appropriate.

"But what does it all signify?" Remi said out loud, expressing her frustration. "If only we had someone who knew more about this."

"Know any astrologers?" Daniel asked. "You pulled a genealogist out of your hat."

"I'm afraid not."

Daniel snapped his fingers. "What about Francesco Costa?"

"The man we found standing over Manetti's body?" Remi glanced at the next table. The woman looked tense enough that Remi felt sure she was listening. Remi couldn't decide whether this amused her or made her feel embarrassed. She decided it did a bit of both.

"Costa would be the perfect person to consult," Daniel said. "We've already cleared him of any wrongdoing, and the death of his colleague will certainly give him motivation to help us. Besides, he's … " Daniel made air quotes, " … the most famous astrologer in Sicily."

Remi chuckled. "You're right. Do we have his number?"

"The Florence police gave it to me. I'll give it to you. Remember he didn't speak much English."

"Don't you speak any Italian?"

A flicker of annoyance ran over Daniel's features. "No."

"Oh, I thought sometimes you were picking up on what people were saying."

"That's just from context and a few similar words," Daniel said, the irritation making it into his voice now.

"Oh, sorry." Remi's apology was automatic. She had stepped on another landmine. But why? That was a puzzle she'd especially like to solve. Costa's number appeared on Remi's phone, giving her a way out of the awkward conversation. “I’ll send Costa the images and see what he has to say.”

As Remi got to work on his phone, Daniel looked through the photos again.

“I hope this guy can come up with something,” Daniel grumbled. “Because I don’t see anything in all of this.”

Costa texted back almost immediately, “A most interesting puzzle! Now I see what my dear departed colleague was so fascinated with. I’ll get to work. I must warn you, however, that a detailed horoscope requires much study and crosschecking and scientific precision. It will take at least a day.”

“He says it will take at least a day,” Remi told Daniel.

“We don’t have a day! Tell him to get his ass in gear.”

“I’ll tell him,” Remi said, typing, “in somewhat more restrained terms.”

“Tell him we’re hunting a killer.”

“He’s aware of that.”

“Is he aware that I’ll kick his ass if he doesn’t get us some answers before our evening gelato?”

“Toxic masculinity will get you nowhere.”

“It has before.” Daniel checked his watch. “Speaking of toxic masculinity, it’s time to talk to Peeters again,” Daniel said, rising, “and this time get some answers.”

* * *

Daniel sauntered into the interrogation room and saw Peeters sitting with an older man with slicked back hair and an expensive suit. This could only be a lawyer. Apparently, they looked the same in every country. You learn something new every day.

A bored-looking policeman stood at the door. Remi came in behind him. She had decided she could be present at police investigations. Not exactly by the book, but the book rarely solved crimes.

The man in the suit stood up and addressed him in careful and correct English.

“I am Binidittu Di Mauro, Signore Peeters’s attorney.”

“I could have guessed. I’m FBI agent Daniel Walker and this is my civilian consultant Remi Laurent. Please sit.”

Daniel decided not to play "bad cop" with this character. He looked sharp, and judging by his stylish suit, in demand.

Di Mauro took the lead. "I have been briefed on the timings of the murders you mentioned and have proof that my client was not present at them."

That was quick.

He pulled out a folder. Inside was a piece of notepaper with several lines written on it in a careful hand. No security camera stills, no receipts, no theater tickets, just a handwritten list.

"Firstly, when you search the flight records you will find that my client was not in either the United States or France at the time of the first two murders. Of course, Florence is a quick drive away, but if he didn't commit the first two murders, there is no reason he would have committed the third."

"He could have hired someone," Daniel said. "And he could have taken the train to France."

The lawyer ignored him.

"Secondly, at the time of the murder in Florence, he was at his local bar watching a sports match. The bartender and several patrons recognized him. He is a regular there. The police already have the bar's contact information. I have not yet had time to gather official statements, but I will.

"Thirdly, while my client did go to Paris when he heard the painting of War by Jan Mertens was for sale, he was outbid by Pierre Lafontaine."

Italo Peeters cut in. "I would have had enough money if that BITCH didn't take half of everything!"

The lawyer shot him the kind of look you give a surly teenager when they say something particularly obnoxious and stupid. "Signor Peeters, please. Let's keep to the matter at hand, shall we?"

"Which is?" Daniel asked. He had the feeling this was going somewhere beyond Peeters being released. At least he hoped so. It looked like they were at yet another dead end.

"Considering the weight of evidence in his favor, my client wishes to be released and given police protection. In return, as an act of good faith, he would like to cooperate with your investigation."

The lawyer said the term "good faith" with a note of irony, as if his client had never done anything in good faith in his entire life.

I was right. This guy is sharp.

"So what can he tell us?" Daniel asked.

The lawyer and Peeters went into a whispering huddle. Once or twice Peeters raised his voice a little, objecting. Di Mauro raised a placating hand and kept on talking. At last, Peeters nodded and turned to them.

"You were right. I did try to buy the painting of War. I lied because I was … afraid." He said this with a screwed-up face, as if the word left a bitter taste in his mouth. "The police, the FBI, Interpol all show up at my door? It took me aback. I heard War was for sale in Paris and I went there to try and purchase it, but Lafontaine paid a better price."

"Did you ever meet Lafontaine?"

Peeters shook his head, looking disappointed. "No. And I didn't try to buy it from him. He paid so much I knew he wouldn't part with it at any price I could afford. So I gave up. And then, just a few days ago, I heard that Pestilence was up for sale. By the time I heard, it had already been snapped up by Pier Paolo Manetti. I called him several times, but he brushed me off."

"Who told you about the paintings being up for sale?" Remi asked.

Peeters continued looking at Daniel as he answered. "I hired an art researcher in Rome to track any sales of paintings. He's quite good. My attorney will supply you with his name so you can check. He found out about the last two sales, but not, sadly the sale of the painting of Death in America."

Hardly surprising, considering the circumstances of that sale, Daniel thought.

He was more inclined to believe Peeters how. He had volunteered information, like the calls to Manetti they already knew about but hadn't confronted him with.

"Did you go to Florence to try and persuade Manetti?" Daniel asked.

"No. He was adamant on the phone. After the fourth or fifth call he became suspicious and asked if I was collecting the paintings too, and if I had one to sell. After that I stopped calling."

"Why were you so eager to reunite the set?"

Peeters eyes glowed with enthusiasm. "You saw them. You know how brilliant they are. The end of the world. Just imagine! The other three paintings were by colleagues—no, friends and fellow travelers!—of my ancestor. How beautiful they would have looked together."

"As beautiful as those paintings of the St. Bartholomew's Day Massacre?" Daniel asked.

His sarcasm was entirely lost on the retired accountant.

"Even more beautiful!" Peeters enthused. "I'm so glad you understand. So few do. When I consented to lend my ancestor's sketches for an exhibition on the massacre, the papers called them 'obscene.' Obscene! Imagine that. And most of the public curled their lips and turned away. I met only one visitor to the exhibition who had the moral courage and aesthetic sense to say they were beautiful."

Daniel blinked. He stared at Peeters for a moment as the man continued to wax lyrical about his ancestor's genius. The words flowed over Daniel unheard as something on the back of his mind began to push its way forward.

"When was this exhibition?"

Peeters looked confused at the question. "Oh, last year."

"Did you exhibit Famine?"

"No. It didn't fit with the theme of the exhibition. Oh, what I wouldn't give for a full retrospective of my—"

"Did any of the publications mention you owned Famine, or were his descendant?"

Peeters puffed out his chest. "Of course. I insisted on it."

Daniel leaned forward, his excitement growing. "And this man who liked the sketches. Tell me about him."

"He was at the opening day. The museum here in Bologna always has a big affair for the opening day of their shows. String quartets, champagne, many of the lenders appear. I wore a tux and—"

"How did this man approach you?"

Peeters, still confused, said, "Well, let me see. The public, who had to pay extra to come on the first day, was mostly from Bologna's smart set. But there was this one man, an American. He had eyes only for my ancestor's work. I do believe I approached him. When I told him who I was, he became most attentive."

Oh, my God. Could this really be?

"What did he look like?"

"Well, about six feet tall. I would say in his early forties. Short blond hair, blue eyes. Strange eyes. They sort of devoured you. Wait, you don't think he is the man who is stealing the paintings?" Peeters turned a shade paler.

Daniel leaned his elbows on the table, getting in close to Peeters.

"Signor Peeters, this is very important. Tell me everything you can remember about this man, and everything you said to him."

They were interrupted by an Italian police officer coming in and whispering in Remi's ear. She then leaned in to whisper in Daniel's.

"They checked with the bartender the lawyer mentioned. He doesn't remember seeing Peeters in the bar. They also checked his phone records for the time of the Paris and New York murders. His phone was in Bologna, turned on but unused."

Daniel bit his lip. Damn. He had just begun to think Peeters might have given them a vital clue to the real murderer, but now suspicion had just been thrown over him again. Bartenders were some of the best witnesses you could ask for. They had a good eye for character and always remembered regulars. Sure, there was a game on, and the bar was probably packed, but Peeters would have ordered a drink or two.

And he hadn't used his phone at the vital times? Given his scintillating personality, the guy was probably a recluse, but he hadn't even checked the Internet? Hadn't used his phone at all?

On the other hand, they didn't have any solid evidence on him.

That slick lawyer gave Daniel the eye.

Damn. He knows something's up. Think quick.

Protective custody is almost as good as arrest. We'll keep him surrounded by cops until we find something to nail this guy with. In the meantime, play along.

"Go get a sketch artist as soon as you can," he told the policeman.

Once the policeman had left, Daniel turned back to the retired accountant. "Please, Signor Peeters. Go on."

"He was a fit man, I remember that. Like someone who had been an athlete in his younger years and had kept in shape even though he was approaching middle age. He spoke quite intelligently about art history and asked all sorts of questions about Frerik Peeters. I … oh." Peters broke out in a sweat. He fumbled for a handkerchief from his pocket and wiped the sweat that had begun to bead on his brow.

"Did you tell him you owned Famine?" Remi asked.

Peeters seemed to be too worried to remember his hatred of women, because he answered quickly, "Yes! Oh God. He's coming after me. But wait, that was six months ago. Why didn't he come after me then? Why is he only killing now?"

"Perhaps the stars are right," Remi said quietly.

Daniel turned to her. "Text that Sicilian astrologer and ask him about that."

Remi got on her phone. Before Daniel could say any more, Peeters's lawyer cut in.

"My client is obviously innocent and obviously in danger. I demand police protection."

Brilliant. He even suggested it himself.

"He'll get it," Daniel said.

The Italian policeman and the lawyer traded some words and the lawyer turned back to Daniel. "He says they will get my client a hotel and post guards."

"I'll be one of them," Daniel said.

The policeman who spoke English came back in. "I'm very sorry, but the sketch artist is out in the city. He says he will return right away but it will take several hours."

"Don't you have another?"

"No."

"Italy is supposed to be the country of artists!"

The policeman looked irritated. "To be a police sketch artist requires special training."

"I'm aware of that. Why haven't you trained more than one person for this whole damn city?"

"The sketch artist can meet him at the hotel."

"Ugh, all right." Daniel turned to Peeters. "We'll take you to that hotel now. Don't worry, we'll keep an eye on you until we get him."

"I must take my painting," Peeters said.

"It would be safer here," Daniel said. He didn't want Peeters anywhere near anything that could be used as evidence at his trial.

"It will be safer with me!"

"You do realize a madman is after it and has already killed to get it."

The cop says to the madman.

Peeters straightened. "Then it's your responsibility to protect us both. I demand police protection."

That took Daniel by surprise. Would the killer really demand the cops watch over him? Perhaps, if he was cunning enough. And the killer had shown himself to be plenty cunning.

"You'll get it, but it would be better to keep the painting here. If you really want to keep it safe—"

Peeters slammed his fist on the table, making his lawyer jump back a little.

"You have no legal right to take my painting. If you take it, I will sue!"

Daniel shrugged. "It's your property. You can do what you like. Don't worry. We'll keep you and Famine safe."

And I won't take my eye off of you, not for anything in the world.

The real question is, how long are you going to be stuck in that hotel until we gather enough evidence against you? And if you're only under protection, we can't cuff you.

That means you're still dangerous.

CHAPTER TWENTY SIX

The Fifth Horseman watched the police station from a bit down the street. That was one of the great things about Italy. There was always a handy outdoor café if you needed to keep an eye on a building. And the Mediterranean culture meant you could savor a wine or two as long as you wanted. No one ever rushed you except at the tourist places.

At last, his patience was rewarded, as he knew it would be. Peeters came out with that American-looking gentleman in the suit, and that European woman, also in civilian clothes. Two Italian policemen accompanied them.

Who were those two? Interpol?

The Fifth Horseman felt a little tremor of fear, quickly suppressed. Such an emotion was unworthy of him.

He rose and turned away quickly, fearful Peeters might recognize him. They were at a distance, and he wore sunglasses and a hat, but it paid to be careful.

The Fifth Horseman had already paid for his drink and snack, so he could leave right away. It was that sort of foresight, that sort of caution, that had gotten him so close to his goal.

The stars were in alignment, and the universe was giving up the paintings one after another. All his predictions were coming true. He was the one fated to decode the Four Horsemen.

The Fifth Horsemen walked quickly, but not too quickly to attract attention, until he got around the corner to where his rental car was parked. Another propitious gift of fate. Finding a parking place in any European city was like winning the lottery.

And it looked like he had lost. There was a parking ticket tucked under his windshield wiper. He cursed himself. He had forgotten to put more money in the meter, so focused he had been on his vigil outside the police station.

This caused him a mild concern as he grabbed the ticket and threw it in the glove compartment. Didn't Son of Sam get caught because of a parking ticket?

Well, the stars had been propitious so far. They had not let him down yet, and they would not let him down now.

He hopped in his car, turned on the ignition, ground the gears in his haste, and sped off, getting to the intersection just as the police passed by. Two police cars. One with Peeters and the plainclothesmen, and another as an escort with two officers.

The Fifth Horseman waited. It made his heart and soul ache to wait, but he waited until another car passed before he got onto the road behind the police cars. It paid to be cautious. The stars might be propitious, but they did not reward fools.

The two patrol cars drove along the narrow two-lane street in downtown Bologna, a little canary yellow Fiat between them and him. He hung back a little.

They got to a yellow light and the patrol cars turned left. The Fiat stopped.

"Damn it!" the Fifth Horseman shouted, banging on the wheel. He craned his neck, trying to see around the corner, but he couldn't.

"How dare he get in the way of my work," he growled.

He felt tempted to get out and kill whoever was in that undersized European car.

He swallowed his rage and waited. While slaughtering that idiot might give short term satisfaction, it would only cause trouble and delay him. He was no psychopath, to kill randomly. He only killed when it furthered his work.

Once he knew the date of the Apocalypse, of course, things would be different. But it would be justified then.

At last, the light changed. The Fiat took what seemed like five thousand years to get into gear and turn. The Fifth Horseman almost honked but stopped himself at the last moment. That would only attract attention.

"Keep cool. Keep cool. You're almost there. Only one more."

The stars smiled on him, as he knew they would. The police cars were still on the same street, almost invisible with three cars between them and him.

Things had turned out better! Now he was less visible. That American-looking man in the suit had looked around suspiciously when he had first arrived at the police station. He was on the watch. He might notice a car following him. Hanging back like this acted as camouflage.

The Fifth Horseman followed them through another couple of turns, always hanging back, always trying to control his impatience. Peeters and the painting were there in the car. He had seen them. So close …

But where were they going? Peeters's apartment was in the other direction.

The answer came soon enough, when the cars went down the ramp into the underground parking lot of the Sheraton.

The Fifth Horseman smiled as he kept driving past the hotel. So they were putting Peeters up in a room, thinking he'd be safe away from home. He'd soon find out differently.

He headed back to his own hotel. Although he had booked five more nights, he would cancel that booking. Too bad about the late cancellation fee. He had found a much more interesting hotel to stay in for his visit to Bologna.

* * *

Remi looked over the arrangements the police had made in the Sheraton and worried. Peeters was sharing a room with Daniel and a lone police officer. The painting was kept in a storage space behind the front desk, watched at all times by a member of hotel staff and a plainclothes policeman posing as a hotel employee. That was done for extra security. If the killer somehow tracked them down, he might go after the painting instead of Peeters. The retired accountant had taken some convincing to separate himself from his precious painting, but even that horrible man saw sense at last. He would be safer this way.

But would he be safe enough? The Italian police felt confident that a change of venue was sufficient. The officer was armed, as was Daniel.

Remi would have liked to have agreed with them, but the last case had made her nervous. The Cryptex Killer had struck again and again, out of the blue and without warning. The man hunting down the Four Horsemen of the Apocalypse showed himself to be equally resourceful. She could not discount the possibility that he would show up.

She wished Torsson was here. Another gun would be good, but he was back at the station, helping run the investigation from that end. The police were following up the records of every tourist in Bologna, a massive list that was taking ages to wade through. Even assuming the killer had American nationality, that left several hundred people.

Remi sat alone in the hotel room next to Peeters's, her phone at her side and her laptop open in front of her as she trawled through the information on the paintings once again, hoping to find something she had missed.

Her phone rang. Francesco Costa, the Sicilian astrologer who had been staying with Pier Paolo Manetti.

"The stars are very bad," he said before she could open her mouth.

"What's wrong?" Remi asked.

"You asked me to look at the stars for today and the last few weeks. Naturally I do that as a matter of course for my work, but now I've taken a second look in light of events. To put it bluntly, if I wanted to commit crimes, now is the time to do it."

Remi tensed. So this was what was egging the killer on, and why he had waited even though he knew Peeters had one of the paintings. He wanted the stars aligned correctly.

"Tell me more," she said.

"Mars in Orion. While it's difficult to see much from the photo of War, I believe Mars is the planet shown in the scholar's book. It's obvious that Orion is the constellation featured in Death. Also, Mars in approaching perigee, the spot in its orbit where it's closest to Earth, and thus it's brighter in the night sky than usual. Also, Venus is close to the Sun and hidden, thus negating her calming influence. The Moon—"

Remi cut him off. She didn't need to know all the pseudoscientific details. "So if you wanted to commit a crime, what day would be the best?"

"Any time in the last month, getting better and better until the end of this week."

Remi let out a long breath she hadn't realized she had been holding. She never thought she'd ever take a horoscope seriously, but the killer did and that was all that mattered.

"Did you get anything from the paintings?" she asked.

"Not much. The photos are too grainy. I'll keep working on it."

"Thank you, Signor Costa."

She hung up. Rising from her place at the hotel room desk, she walked over to the window. Night had fallen. The hotel had been cheap, and their view was of nothing but an office building, now dark. The good views were on the other side of the hotel, looking out over Bologna's skyline and those towers Daniel was so oddly engaged with. Strange fellow. So rough and so hypersensitive at the same time.

Thinking of her partner made her think of Cyril. He still hadn't called or texted, and that left a hollow loneliness inside her that felt bottomless.

She grabbed her phone. Still no message. *Damn him.*

Before she could think, she texted him. She had promised herself that she wouldn't, but she found her fingers flying across the screen.

"In Bologna and still on the case. We might be close to solving it. I'll give you a call when I know when I'm coming back."

She paused, finger hovering over the Send button.

Then she went back and deleted "give you a call" and replaced it with "notify." More neutral and businesslike. It showed she was still angry.

She had to keep that much of her pride at least.

The response came almost instantly.

"Glad to hear you're safe. We'll talk more when you're free."

Remi's heart leapt. That he had responded so quickly showed he felt bad about their fight. The neutral-sounding message was just his way of soothing his pride. But even that expressed that he wanted to talk.

It would have been nice if there had been a "sorry" in there somewhere.

He's a middle-aged man who went through a bad divorce and is worried he won't ever get married again. Go easy on him.

Well, he wouldn't have to worry about that so much if he went easy on me.

Her fingers hesitated over the screen, trying to formulate a reply.

A text came in from Daniel. She opened it.

"All good over here except the company. I feel like killing this guy myself. How are you?"

Remi smiled. She imagined him falling asleep as Peeters droned on and on about his not-so-famous ancestor and his own theories of art. Poor man. She'd leave that job to him. Peeters didn't want to talk to her anyway.

She texted back, "Better you than me."

She got a crying emoji in return. That made her laugh.

Just then the lights went out.

CHAPTER TWENTY SEVEN

Remi turned on the flashlight on her phone and rushed to the door of her room.

She got into the hallway just as Daniel opened his door. They ended up shining their flashlights in each other's faces.

"Ah! Get that out of my eyes!" she said.

"You do the same," Daniel said, putting his hand over his face. Remi saw he was holding his gun, no doubt drawn the instant he was left in the darkness with Peeters. Remi couldn't blame him. She sure wouldn't want to be in a dark room with that worm.

"What's going on?" Peeters demanded from inside the room.

Daniel turned to him. "Just sit tight, Signor Peeters. You, Antonio, go down and see what's happening while I stay with him. Our man downstairs isn't picking up."

"All right," the Italian officer said in English.

"Check on the painting," Remi added in Italian.

The man nodded and walked quickly for the stairs at the end of the hall, a flashlight in his hand.

"Go back in the room and sit tight; I can handle Peeters. Don't worry, I won't take my eyes off him. Or my gun," Daniel told Remi, then closed the door.

Remi shook her head. How many times had he told her that and how many times had it worked? Americans never learned.

She slammed her room door, knowing that Daniel would hear it, and followed the police officer down the hall. He had just passed through the door to the stairs and gone out of sight.

By the time she got to the door to the stairwell, he had made it a couple of floors down. He stood there, telling a worried couple to go back to their rooms. Remi watched as the lights from their phones disappeared and the policeman continued down the stairs, his flashlight beam bobbing back and forth in time to his steps.

Remi followed. He probably heard her but wouldn't have thought anything of someone else on the stairwell. He didn't look up, anyway.

He disappeared through the ground floor door. Remi hastened down the rest of the stairwell.

As she got to the door, caution kicked in. She turned off her phone, plunging the stairwell into near darkness. Each landing had a narrow window, but as it faced a nearby office building, closed for the evening, it let in little light.

Remi opened the door a crack. From what she could see, it opened into a hallway. To her left was a glass door leading to a dining area, visible thanks to its large windows overlooking a garden she had remembered seeing when she arrived. To her right the hallway led to the front desk area. She could see little out there, as the hallway made a right turn. Faint light, no doubt from the streetlights shining through the glass front doors, shone from around the corner.

She slipped out into the hallway. A cry and the thud of a body hitting the floor made her pause. Someone shouted. The sound of running feet, then an agonized scream.

Run, her instincts told her. *It's only a painting. Let the police handle it.*

She didn't listen. The Remi Laurent of six months ago would have listened. She would have taken the safe, sane option. But now, after having had a taste of the chase on not one but two cases, she couldn't turn back.

She moved forward, clutching her pepper spray.

More sound of movement around the corner, and an agonized gasp, followed by heavy breathing.

Creeping to the corner, she peeked around.

All she saw was the front desk of the hotel. The lobby was empty, dimly lit by the streetlights filtering inside through the big glass doors.

Where is everyone?

Another moan. The sound of movement behind the counter.

Not daring to turn on the flashlight on her phone, she crouched down and crept out of sight along the front desk to where it was open on one side, allowing the employees to get behind it.

The painting had been placed in a locker in the room behind.

She peeked around the open portion of the counter. Dimly she could see the shapes of two bodies, lying prone, dark blots in the general gloom. One shifted slightly, emitting a moan. Where was the third man? There had been the receptionist, the plainclothesman, and the uniformed officer she had followed down. But she saw only two bodies.

A crash in the back room made her jump. Briefly a faint light flicked on back there. She got a fleeting image of the doorway, a row of suitcases lined against the wall, and that was all.

She crept behind the counter, peering at the two figures. Now that she was closer, she could tell one was the policeman. He was unconscious or dead. The other was dressed in a suit. Guest? Manager? The plainclothes officer? She couldn't tell. He moaned softly, his leg shifting a little.

The back room lit up briefly again, and she saw the little will-o'-wisp on a penlight dance briefly at the far end of the room before winking out.

Remi crouched there in the shadows, unsure what to do. She shifted to the right, intending on getting to the side of the doorway and out of sight until she could figure out her course of action, but as she did so her foot struck something small and heavy on the floor. There was a metallic clatter and a thump as whatever she had kicked hit the back of the counter.

The pen light snapped back on, fixing her in its beam.

Remi let out a little cry and froze.

"Don't worry, ma'am," an American voice said. "I'm trying to find the main fuse box. What's going on around here? Someone hurt that cop and the manager and then ran upstairs."

Blinking in the light that still shone on her, Remi gripped her pepper spray and replied, "I-I don't know."

Is this him? Or did he run upstairs?

The killer might have beaten up the manager to get Peeters's room number.

Remi turned on the flashlight on her phone, illuminating the scene.

A well-built man about six feet tall stood in the back room. To one side, the door to the lockup was open. She could see the painting leaning against the back wall. The man stood at the other side of the back room. This made her breathe a bit easier.

What made her pause was that he still kept the pen light pointed directly at her, held at head level so she couldn't see his face.

"Ah! Thanks, ma'am. There's the fuse box."

He walked over to the little metal panel on one wall.

I need to call Daniel. But to do that I have to take my eyes off him. He's only a few steps away.

The sound of a fist pounding on glass made her jump.

She whirled around and saw an Italian couple standing outside the sliding glass door, knocking on the glass and peering into the darkened lobby. The automatic door was stuck shut thanks to the electricity being out.

Immediately she whirled back around to keep an eye on the American, half expecting to find him rushing for her.

But he was still fiddling with the fuse box.

"Someone's smashed the main switch," he said. "I can't get it back on. What the hell is going on?"

Perhaps it was the confidence in his voice. Perhaps it was the fact that the closet lay open and he hadn't grabbed the painting. Perhaps it was the persistent knocking on the glass door by the Italian couple, assuring her she wasn't alone.

Perhaps it was all three things. Whatever it was, Remi never quite knew, but she felt enough confidence to tuck the pepper spray in her breast pocket and call Daniel.

And before it even had a chance to ring, Remi froze. Because the man fussing with the fuse panel had lowered his pen light a little, and Remi could see he looked in his forties, athletic and with short blond hair and blue eyes.

Just as Peeters described the man who had spoken to him about his paintings.

"Hello?" Daniel's voice came over the phone.

The man turned to her, a strange light coming into his gaze. Remi looked away, trying to act casual. The knocking at the glass door continued.

Remi spotted what she had accidentally kicked a minute before.

The policeman's gun, lying a couple of steps away against the inside of the counter.

"Front desk!" she shouted into the phone.

She tossed the phone at the killer, startling him for a moment as she dove for the gun.

Diving down, she grasped the pistol, a long-barreled .38. Much like the one her father used to let her fire in the countryside. Although she hadn't fired one since she was a teenager.

She sure would fire one now.

If she got the chance. The killer hadn't stayed startled for long. He tossed aside his own pen light and rushed her, hands reaching out.

She brought the gun up. Too late.

His hand clamped like iron on her wrist, pushing her aim away. His other hand went behind his back, pulled out something from under his shirt, and came back into view.

The streetlight filtering through the glass door was just enough for Remi to see the gleam of a knife.

"You didn't recognize me in time," the killer said. "But I recognized you. Oh yes, I recognized you from Peeters's house, and again at the police station. I was hoping to bluff you into going away so I wouldn't have to bother with you. But no, you stayed. You're getting in my way. No one does that and lives."

CHAPTER TWENTY EIGHT

Remi's entire body went cold. All she could do was stare at the knife poised inches from her face. She still held the gun, but her hand was imprisoned by a strong grip. She couldn't even move her wrist to angle the gun at him.

"Drop it," he ordered.

"You'll never get away. You'll—"

"Drop it." His grip tightened, making Remi hiss in pain.

A light shone on them. "What the hell!"

They both turned to see a startled American tourist standing nearby, a real one this time.

They were just as startled as he was.

For a moment the three of them stared at one another, frozen.

The Daniel burst in on the scene, gun drawn, and elbowed the American tourist out of the way.

"Freeze!" he ordered. "Drop the knife and let her go!"

"We need to know the time!" the killer shouted, then crouched, putting the counter and Remi between him and Daniel's line of fire.

At the same time, he smacked Remi's wrist against the counter, making the gun go off. Remi cried out, both in pain and in fear. The gun had been pointing roughly at Daniel.

The killer smacked her wrist a second time and the pistol fell on the opposite side of the counter. Then the man, still wielding his knife, leapt over the counter at Daniel.

There was a loud report as Daniel's gun went off, then the thud of two bodies hitting each other.

Remi tried to see what was going on in the half light. The Italian couple still stood at the glass door as if hypnotized. The American tourist had fled. The killer and Daniel rolled around on the floor. The killer got on top and started pounding Daniel with his fist.

She had to get that gun. Remi vaulted over the counter.

At least that was her intention. A lifetime of historical research hadn't made her particularly good at vaulting over counters.

She stumbled, fell hard on her knees, losing a moment as pain spiked through her legs.

When she looked up, the killer was already advancing, knife in hand, Daniel lying motionless on the floor behind him.

Remi saw the gun lying just out of reach to her left. She ducked for it.

The killer was quicker. Just as her fingers touched the grip, he placed his foot on it.

Remi looked up at the man towering over her. He glared down at her, fire in his eyes. Blood trickled down the side of his head. Daniel had shot part of his ear off.

Swallowing with a throat suddenly gone dry, she slowly stood.

"You said you needed to know the time," she croaked. "You mean the time of the Apocalypse?"

The killer smiled, the most frightening expression he could have possibly made in that situation.

"Oh yes. We'll know when humanity will be wiped from the face of the Earth. Won't it be glorious?"

"But what if it's not now?"

His free hand whipped out like lightning and grasped her throat. He did not press, did not choke. He merely kept her immobile.

"Then I'll just have to speed things up."

Remi knew he was about to kill her, so she did the only thing she could do, even if it meant her death. She would not go down without a fight, and she would not go down without hurting this maniac and perhaps aiding his capture.

She reached for the pepper spray in her pocket. The killer, sensing the movement, turned his head to see what she was doing.

No time to pull the little bottle from her pocket. All she could do was aim it up, screw her eyes shut, and spray.

Her face immediately began to burn, followed a moment later by her chest as the spray leaked through her blouse.

She heard the killer gag. The grip on her wrist loosened for a moment. She brought the gun around and fired.

At the last second, he jerked her hand away.

Then the grip released. Had she hit him?

A moment later she got slapped upside the head, making her stumble to the side. By instinct she opened her eyes.

Immediately she felt a searing pain. Her sight wavered as tears welled up in them. The light vanished as the tourist stopped shining his phone on them, probably busy running away.

Remi didn't have time to check. The killer stood not two yards away, stumbling around and wiping his eyes, trying to focus on her, a maniacal rage keeping him on his feet.

She had to stop him now. She'd be blind in a few seconds.

Remi crouched, grabbed the gun, and fired just as she took a bad lungful of pepper spray and let out a spasmodic cough. Her gun bucked as it went off.

The last she saw was a vague shadow falling.

* * *

Remi sat in the back of an ambulance as an EMT poured saline solution on her eyes. They were as red and swollen as that hippie student in her Medieval Folklore class, but at least she could see again.

Daniel had arrived a few moments after she shot the killer. He had subdued him, turned the on the fuses—which of course hadn't been destroyed—, found the plainclothes officer lying unconscious and out of sight in the storage closet, and called for backup. Now he stood by her, a worried expression on his face.

At least she thought he had a worried expression. She still had trouble focusing. He certainly sounded worried.

"How are you feeling?" he asked for the tenth time.

"Slightly less miserable than I felt a minute ago. Thank you for asking again."

"The other ambulances just left," he told her. "The manager and the two cops will be just fine, although they're all going to need stitches. The killer knocked him them out instead of stabbed them. I guess he didn't want to make noise."

"I'm glad they'll be OK. And the killer?"

She found her heart start beating faster. Daniel hadn't mentioned anything about him. All she knew was that he was alive and in custody.

"You shot him in the leg."

Remi let out breath of relief. She did not want someone's death on her hands, not even someone like that.

"Nice shooting for someone who was blinded by her own pepper spray," Daniel added.

"Thanks. God, this stuff burns. My skin feels like it's on fire."

"Maybe that'll keep you from pepper spraying everyone you meet," Daniel said with a chuckle.

"Maybe I should meet nicer people."

"No chance on this job. You wouldn't believe what I found on him."

"What?"

"Handcuffs, a needle and thread, and a straw."

Remi's brow furrowed. That caused odd horizontal lines of pain across her brow, so she unfurrowed it. "The handcuffs I understand if he wanted to capture Peeters, but what was he doing with the other things?"

"Famine," Daniel whispered. "He was going to handcuff Italo Peeters somewhere isolated and sew his lips shut so he couldn't eat. The straw was so he could give Peeters water. To fit the pattern, he needed to starve to death, not die of thirst. And he would have had to stay there watching, for the better part of a month, before Peeters finally succumbed."

The EMT treating Remi showed her knowledge of English by gasping.

"Famine," Remi said, and shuddered. "What a horrible fate."

"If anyone deserves it, it would be Peeters. Still, it's our job to protect the public, even if the public includes slime balls."

"Hitting his wife deserves a prison sentence, not a death sentence."

"I wasn't referring to the wife," Daniel said, his voice growing distant.

"Well, it's all over now," she reassured him, although she wasn't quite sure what he was reassuring him about.

"It's never over," he grumbled. "At least this case is closed. After some debriefings and a mountain of paperwork, we should be able to fly home by the end of the week."

"I think I'll stay in Italy for a few more days."

Daniel turned to her, surprised. "Why?"

Remi felt herself flush. She still hadn't told him of her continuing research into the cryptex.

"After all that's happened, I need a bit of a vacation." That at least, was true enough.

“I can imagine. I’m sure my boss will understand. I think she likes you. I’ll tell her you need to let off some stress here. You won’t be on FBI expenses, though.”

Remi smiled. “Good. I can stay in a decent hotel them.”

Daniel laughed. “Just for that I’ll fix things with your dean. All I have to do is not tell him you’re done with the case. He’s got people covering your classes?”

“Yes.”

“It’s all set then. Enjoy your vacation.”

It won’t be a vacation, but I will enjoy it.

* * *

The next morning, Remi sat, fascinated, in the archive in Florence. The archaeological report was there just like she knew it would be, and it told her so much.

For here, in detailed description and a large map, was the entire layout of the Church of Saint Pantaleon of Nicomedia.

The archaeologists had performed an excavation in 2007 as part of a provincial project across Tuscany delving into the foundations of lesser-known churches. While most of the famous churches of the region had been thoroughly examined over the years, Tuscany had so many medieval and Renaissance churches that many had never been properly studied by archaeologists, even though architects and art historians had examined every inch of every church. Archaeological investigations were expensive and intrusive.

So the regional government of Tuscany got some money from UNESCO to perform test excavations into each church to determine when they were founded. While many records existed for the churches, often with detailed accounts of their funding and initial construction, other records were missing; and often the records that did exist didn’t mention earlier buildings on the site. The idea of the project was to see the pattern of church building from the earliest days of legal Christianity in the late Roman Empire through the Middle Ages, Renaissance, and Early Modern period.

In the case of the Church of Saint Pantaleon of Nicomedia, the archaeologists found something quite interesting.

The church was supposedly built in the 13th century, shortly before the cryptex itself had been constructed. Test excavations in the nave and apse, however, uncovered the foundations of a smaller 8th century church, and below that a tiny chapel from the fourth century that could have been any sort of building except that, on the last day of the excavation, the archaeologists found a portion of wall tile showing a fish, the symbol of Jesus.

A little prickle ran up Remi's spine as she looked at the photo. The artifact itself wasn't much to look at, a chipped ceramic tile with an incised fish made of two simple lines, much like the symbols American Christians put on the rear bumpers of their cars. But that little design proved the Late Roman building to be a chapel, and that there had been an unbroken chain of Christian worship at the Church of Saint Pantaleon of Nicomedia for at least 1,700 years.

This is what hooked her into historical research, these sorts of discoveries. She suspected the archaeologists had felt the same way.

Then why not publish their findings? She had done an extensive Internet search of the church and had found no mention of the excavation except a brief article in a local paper about the commencement of the project. Nothing about its findings. This was a big enough discovery that it should have made at least regional, if not national, news.

After having made a general overview of the report, she focused on the section where the archaeologists described their findings in the nave.

The map hidden inside the cryptex had an X marking a spot halfway down the nave. Remi had worried the excavators might have already found what she sought.

She could breathe easy on that score. Since their first test pit, just outside the church walls on the west end of the building, had discovered the foundations of the 8th century church, they had focused their excavations on that side. Inside the church they had sunk a test pit in the apse and in the nave close to the apse, but not halfway down the nave at the spot she was interested in.

These excavations had revealed parts of the two earlier churches. To be thorough, the team had also sunk a test pit at the eastern end of the apse but had found no earlier structures.

Her spot had not been disturbed.

They had also made a general survey of the building itself and noted that the nave had been "all but unchanged since the 14th century except for the addition of a pair of side chapels in the 16th century."

Remi took in a sharp inhalation of breath. “All but unchanged.” Perfect. There was a chance that whatever the cryptex map had marked might still be there.

Only one way to find out. Remi pulled out her phone and called a car rental agency. She’d go to the church right away.

CHAPTER TWENTY NINE

The Church of Saint Pantaleon of Nicomedia stood on a low rise just above a village, a scattering of small houses extending down the slope on either side of a narrow lane. Behind the church stood a forest. A few miles away, a lake, created thanks to the dam project by Mussolini in the late twenties, glittered at the bottom of the slope.

On the shores of the lake stood a large town ringed with the remnants of a medieval city wall. In its center rose the spire of its own, grander church. The Church of Saint Pantaleon of Nicomedia, whatever its position in earlier times, now probably only served the village and the occasional traveler.

Remi felt a sense of profound relief. The best-preserved churches were those that got passed over by history, the ones that got sidelined by newer, grander churches and never saw much expansion or restoration over the years. The original fabric on such churches got preserved. According to the archaeological report, the addition of side chapels in the 16th century had been the only major modification to the church. Certainly, there had been minor restorations—a new altar for the chapel in one century, the replacement of a broken stained glass window in another century—but she hoped she'd find the church more or less intact from the time of the cryptex.

She hoped.

While she was the first, as far as she knew, to open the cryptex, there was no telling how many people had poked and probed around the church over the years. Bandits, looting soldiers, treasure hunters, any number of people might have stumbled upon whatever was hidden on the space marked X on the cryptex map.

And then there was the Catholic Church itself. They had bought the cryptex from the museum where it had been hidden. While they did not have the key to opening it like Remi had, they had two thousand years of knowledge and expertise backing them up. They might have solved the cryptex already and come here to claim the prize.

And then there was the shadowy Order of St. Adrian of Nicomedia. She had met one of its initiates during the Cryptex Killer case. He hadn't spoken much, but she had learned that his group was a religious order that vowed to protect the cryptex and its secret.

Had they, perhaps, come here before her? The church had many factions, and they might not have wanted the current administration in the Vatican to claim the cryptex. They might have their own reasons to keep its secret hidden for the time being.

As Remi drove slowly through the village and uphill toward the church, her heart beating fast in anticipation of finally reaching her goal, she did not consider that she should honor the order's wishes. Or the Vatican's, for that matter. She was a scholar, although she realized with satisfaction that she was a detective now too. But first and foremost, she was a scholar, and as such she had a devotion to knowledge. Nothing should be hidden. Like an investigative journalist who uncovers secret corruption and cabals in the highest levels of government, she was a tireless researcher trying to unlock the secrets of history.

There was a small plaza in front of the church. Only a couple of other cars were parked there. Remi had timed her arrival to avoid any services. Hopefully no tour buses showed up. In Italy they could pop up out of nowhere at the most inopportune times, although she doubted this out-of-the-way church was on any tour company's itinerary.

She parked and took a good look around as she got out of her rental car. Like most rural Italian villages during the daytime, the main street was deserted. The younger residents would be at school or work in the larger town by the lake, the very same one marked on the cryptex all those centuries ago. Some others might be working the fields in the surrounding countryside. The older residents would be sitting at home, or in the small park further down the slope that she had passed a couple of minutes before.

Good. The fewer people who saw her, the better.

Tucking her heavy purse under her arm, she heard the tools inside clank against each other.

Remi cursed quietly to herself.

I thought I'd wrapped them up well enough. Maybe I should get back in the car and do it again.

She hesitated, reached for her keys, then stopped.

You're procrastinating. No one is going to stop you for having a rattling purse. Get in there and find what you came for.

Taking a deep breath and standing a little straighter, she headed for the church. She walked far too quickly, her gait stiff and rapid.

Relax. The more you relax the less noticeable you will be.

How many outsiders come to this church?

It doesn't matter. Remember the story you made up. You took a wrong turn out of town, saw the lovely church on the hill, and decided to visit.

While her mind ran through all the terrible ways this could all go wrong, her expert gaze ran over the front of the church.

The front was classic 14th century, with an arched Gothic doorway, its heavy wooden door worryingly shut, and above that a pretty rose window of stained glass. The gabled roof had three little turrets, one on the peak and one on each side. At the far end of the church rose the bell tower, with a gold cross gleaming from its domed roof. The entire construction looked much like a miniature version of the Santa Maria Gloriosa dei Frari near Venice.

She reached out for the heavy iron ring at the door, turned, and pushed.

To her relief, it creaked open.

She stepped inside, eyes adjusting to the dim light as her nostrils filled with the smell of burning wax and incense.

Remi closed the door behind her, and in her nervousness misjudged the distance and shut it with a loud slam.

She gritted her teeth. So much for subtlety.

Quickly she looked around, imagining an angry priest striding up to her, a scowl on his face and a finger on his lips. Then he'd follow her around, never giving her a chance to examine the church properly or discover its prize.

Luckily no such thing happened. Remi could only see one person in the pews, an old woman dressed all in black, head bowed in prayer with a few gray hairs peeking out from around her black kerchief.

The woman was so concentrated on her prayers that she didn't even turn around. Or perhaps she had fallen asleep.

Remi moved quietly down the side of the nave; her arm pressed tightly against her purse so the tools inside would not rattle.

She pulled out her phone and took a panning video of the church as an excuse to linger and look around. The interior was typical of the period, with tall walls of gray stone blocks reaching up to a high Gothic arch. The walls were punctuated with stained glass windows showing scenes from the Bible and the lives of the saints, the light passing through them dappling the pews with patterns of color.

On the far end stood an ornate Rococo altar that looked late 18th century. Its flowery gilt decoration with cherubs blowing trumpets and angels soaring on their wings looked gauche next to the restrained beauty of the rest of the church. Remi imagined some nouveau riche merchant, eager to show off his wealth, donating this visual travesty to the church, not realizing that generations of artistically sensitive visitors would sneer at his poor taste.

Remi almost laughed. Daniel would have made some half-serious mocking comments about her snobbery. She wished he was here, sharing in this discovery. It would have intrigued him, especially after he put his life on the line recovering the cryptex. Not for the first time, she regretted her decision not to tell him about opening it.

That regret had never been enough to change her mind. What she had done was illegal, as was what she planned to do. If the creators of the cryptex had left something hidden in this church, she planned to take it. That was theft, plain and simple. Her only justification for this plainly wrong act was that no one knew the object was here.

Assuming it really was an object. She turned her gaze to the walls. Oil paintings of religious figures, darkened with time and dust, hung every few feet. She dismissed these as possibilities. Most of these paintings dated to later centuries, and those that weren't could have easily been moved. It was the stone carvings that intrigued her.

Typical in Gothic churches, there were massive porphyry columns set into the walls to help bear the weight of the arched ceiling. These had ornate capitals where they met the base of the arch, with grinning gargoyles and saintly abbots staring down at the congregation.

She walked slowly along. The spot she wanted was situated on the south side of the nave about halfway along. She wished the map had been more precise. While this wasn't a big church, it was big enough. The keepers of the cryptex secret must have felt that once the seeker knew the general location, the exact spot would be obvious.

She hoped it would be obvious to her.

There.

Remi stopped, a slight gasp escaping her throat.

For there on the wall, right at head level, was a carving of the Shield of the Trinity.

It was a triangle about the size of her splayed hand with its base at the top. At the two top corners were circles with the words "Pater" and "Filius," "Father" and "Son." At the bottom corner was a circle with the inscription "Spiritus Sanctus," the "Holy Spirit." Connecting the three corners were bars inscribed with "non est," or "isn't." In the center of the triangle was a circle marked "Deus" for "God", with bars connecting each of the corners to it with the word "est" for "is."

The Shield of the Trinity was a common method of showing the concept of the three-in-one nature of God. It could be easily read that "The Father is not the Son is not the Holy Spirit" and "The Father is God, the Son is God, the Holy Spirit is God." Three aspects of Godhood, separate and distinct but also united and indivisible. A difficult concept struggled over by centuries of theologians and laypeople, explained in a simple diagram.

Remi stared. This carving was on the right spot marked in the cryptex map. She stared at it, feeling lightheaded. Then she got herself together and looked around a bit more, checking if there were any other features nearby that could be what she sought.

She saw none. In fact, this appeared to be the only carving in the church within reach of someone standing on the floor.

This is it. This is really it.

But now what?

She stared at it, uncertain what to do next. This was just a carving on the wall. There were no shelves nearby, no keyholes, nothing.

Glancing over her shoulder to make sure no one was watching, she peered closer at the carving. The light inside the church was dim, despite the stained glass windows and the candles, but did she see a seam running around each of the three circles on the corners?

Remi pushed on one. It didn't budge. She pushed on the other two with the same lack of result.

She pushed harder. Nothing.

Perhaps they had to be pushed in a pattern, like the cryptex had to be opened with a pattern?

Of course! What had been the code to open the cryptex? D3IS1.

She had taken that to mean in Latin, "Dios 3 Iesvs 1." Or "God 3 Jesus 1."

Daniel would probably make some quip about dads beating sons at football, but of course he knew the significance as well as she did. God as part of the Trinity, Jesus as the one path to God.

And that's exactly what this carving symbolized.

But what was she supposed to do next?

She glanced around. There had been two cars parked outside the church, and she doubted that lone old woman still praying in the pews had driven herself up here. So there were at least two other people around somewhere.

But where?

A priest and a member of the congregation in the confessional? A couple of lay volunteers doing some work in one of the private chambers? Whoever they were, they could appear at any time.

If they saw some strange woman, obviously not a member of the congregation with her French accent and clothes, fiddling with the carving, they might intervene.

She couldn't let that happen.

Controlling her impatience, she quickly walked around the rest of the church to find out where the other people were. As she suspected, she found two older women dusting the altar in one of the 16th century side chapels. The altar wasn't as in such poor taste as the main altar, but it still jarred with the main Gothic ambience of the church.

Remi paused a moment, watching. The two volunteers, busy with their work, did not notice her.

Remi hurried away before they did. It looked like they'd be occupied for a while. The old woman in black was shuffling for the door. Now was her chance.

Getting back to the Shield of the Trinity, Remi took a deep breath, wiped her brow, and thought for a moment.

God three, Jesus one.

Remi pressed on the central circle marked "Deus." Then she pressed on all three circles on the corners of the triangle, having to stretch one hand to use her thumb and pinky finger. Had she felt a slight shift in the circles, or was that her imagination?

Next, she pressed the circle marked "Filius."

Nothing happened.

Jesus one.

Jesus is God.

She pressed the circle marked "Deus" again.

There was a soft click, and a creak as a panel of stone slightly larger than the triangle opened a little.

Remi hooked her nails on the edge to open it further.

“Excuse me,” a voice said behind her.

CHAPTER THIRTY

Remi swung around, a frantic excuse caught in her throat. Before her stood a rotund little priest wearing thick glasses.

Before she could form words, the priest said in Italian, "Welcome to our church. Are you visiting from far away?"

"Um," Remi coughed. "Yes. I'm French. I teach art at an, um, private school for teenagers. I love Gothic architecture and I wanted to visit your church since it has many well preserved features. Remarkable, isn't it? Such fine carvings on the column capitals. And that baptismal font? Beautiful! It's, ah … "

Remi realized she was babbling and stopped.

The priest smiled. "It's so nice to meet a foreigner visitor. We don't get many. And one who speaks lovely Italian too!" Then he gestured behind her, making her heart clench. "And what's this?"

Remi almost fainted. "Oh! It's … "

Desperately she tried to formulate an excuse for why she had suddenly opened up a mysterious panel in the wall of this man's church. Before she could come up with anything, he went on.

"This is called the Shield of the Trinity. It is an illustration of the doctrine of the Trinity and how the Father, Son, and Holy Spirit are separate but one."

"Um, right."

"It would be a good thing to show your schoolchildren. Perhaps you should take a photo of it."

Remi searched for irony or menace in the priest's tone and found none. Then it hit her—with those Coke bottle glasses, he couldn't see the Shield of the Trinity was slightly ajar. He thought she was merely admiring the carving!

Her knees almost buckled in relief. "Oh, yes! That's a splendid idea!"

She pulled out her phone so quickly that the tools inside her purse rattled loudly.

The priest chuckled. "Sounds like you overburdened yourself with souvenirs at the gift shop in town."

"Something like that."

"Well, enjoy your visit."

The priest walked away down the apse and disappeared into the side chapel where the volunteers were no doubt still cleaning.

Remi stood for a moment, catching her breath and getting a hold of herself. Then the drive for discovery overtook her once again and, after giving another cautious look around her, she grasped the edge of the panel and pulled.

It swung open to reveal a small shelf inset into the wall. On that shelf was a ceramic statuette about six inches tall of the Virgin Mary holding the baby Jesus.

She plucked it out, tucked it in her purse, and closed the panel.

In her hurry, the stone slammed shut, the heavy sound echoing through the building.

"Why do these places have to have such good acoustics?" Remi grumbled, heading for the door.

She didn't make it.

The priest popped out of the side chapel, squinting around for the source of the sound.

"I bumped my shin on one of the pews," she called over. "Silly me. I was admiring the ceiling and not watching where I was going."

"Are you all right?" the priest asked in a soft voice that barely carried over to her. His tone suggested she lower her volume. Remi did.

"Yes," she said so softly she wasn't sure it carried over to him. "Sorry."

He nodded and disappeared into the side chapel again.

Remi hurried for the door.

Just before opening it, she stopped. A donation box stood next to it, an old chest of aged wood with heavy iron bands around it and a slit in the top. It looked like it had been sitting there for hundreds of years, accepting the donations of the faithful.

Suddenly, Remi felt guilty. She had just robbed this church. While she had taken something they didn't know they had made it somewhat easier, it was still theft.

She rummaged in her purse, digging past the figurine and wrenches and chisels and hammers to extract her wallet.

Remi pulled out a ten euro note and stuck it in the collection box. Pausing, she pulled out a twenty and put that in too. She started to put her wallet away, hesitated, then pulled it out again.

She removed every note and put it in the collection box, then pulled out her change purse and emptied its contents into the box too.

Does that make you feel better? She asked herself.

Yes. A bit.

Does that make what you just did right?

No. Not really. But I have to. And in the larger scheme of human knowledge, it is the right thing to do.

She thought about that as she went to her car and, after an inner struggle, decided it was true.

* * *

Back at her hotel room in Bologna she stared at the figurine. It was a simple thing, not terribly well made, the kind of ceramic figurine pressed out of clay in a mold and fired to hardness before being sold by the hundreds to pilgrims and churchgoers. Some were painted. This one was not. Stylistically, she judged it to be 13th century, the same time the cryptex was made.

An unremarkable artifact, except for two important features.

One, the cryptex had pointed her to it.

And two, it rattled.

Remi remembered the plaster bust of the historian Edward Gibbon in the Glencairn Museum that hid a copper cylinder inside with a note, and the ivory statue of the Virgin Mary at the Cloisters, which had also contained a note.

Could this little clay figurine contain a note baked in when it was made?

Remi turned it over in her hands. There was no seam, no hole, no way to get inside. She pressed on every surface, hoping to spring a catch and pop it open, like she had with the wall at the Church of Saint Pantaleon of Nicomedia.

No luck. It was fired as one piece, whatever it contained being sealed inside.

I have to break it.

The realization made her pause. This figurine was more than 700 years old!

No other way to get inside. They intended for you to break it.

Yes, when it was new, not when it was a valuable antique.

It's not valuable, or rare. You can buy one on eBay for a few hundred dollars.

It's still an antique.

Remi groaned and stood up from her hotel room desk.

Pacing back and forth, she went over and over the problem in her mind. The figurine obviously contained the final cryptex revelation, or at least another clue to the revelation, which had laid hidden for centuries. The only way to uncover it was to smash the figurine.

But she couldn't do that. She was an art historian, for God's sake!

Art historians don't rob churches.

Remi stopped, letting out a deep sigh. She had come this far, compromised so many of her professional ethics, she couldn't exactly stop now.

And, deep in her heart, from the moment she had discovered the figurine she had known she'd do what she was about to do.

At least I've photographed and measured it thoroughly, making a complete record for posterity. And maybe I can minimize the damage.

Remi fetched a pair of pliers from her purse.

Sitting back down at the desk, she picked up the figurine and set the pliers on either side of the Virgin Mary's feet.

Is this a sin? I'm not a Catholic but I'm pretty sure this is a sin.

Except that the Catholic church, or some faction within it, made this figurine specifically to be broken.

That made her feel better. Sort of.

She gently pressed down on the pliers, wincing as she heard a crack. A hairline fracture ran halfway up the figurine. The bottom did not snap off as she wanted it to, however.

She had to press harder, so shc did.

The entire figurine shattered into a dozen pieces.

"Damn it!"

Her anger at her clumsiness evaporated as a small copper cylinder tumbled to the desktop along with the figurine fragments.

A chill ran down her spine. Putting down the pliers quietly, as if nervous about disturbing her new find, she gently picked it up.

It was a small copper tube about the size of a cigarette, closed at both ends. She shook it gently and heard the sound of something moving a bit inside. Her instinct told her it was a rolled-up piece of paper or something similar.

Remi pulled out a pair of wire cutters from her purse. When she had gone to a hardware store in Florence the previous day, she had felt crazy buying all these tools, not knowing which she'd need in the church, if any at all. Now they were coming in handy.

With breathless care, she put the wire cutters on the very end of the copper tube, angled the tube a bit so whatever was inside would sink to the other end, and pressed.

The end of the tube popped off with a loud snip.

Remi took a deep breath, set down the wire cutters, and cupped her hand, turning the copper tube so the open side hung down.

A little roll of parchment fell into her hand.

Trembling a little, she tried to unroll it.

Her hands shook too much. She fumbled the paper and it popped out of her grasp. She gave a little yelp as it almost rolled off the table.

She grabbed it, took a deep breath to settle herself, and carefully unrolled it.

Written on it, in a small and tidy hand, was a series of letters and numbers.

"X3f6Oee7c7
bE336ungl2
6phoistmil"

A code.

Disappointment threatened to drag her down. She'd searched for so long, risked and compromised so much, only to be confronted with another puzzle.

But then a slow smile spread across Remi's face.

Oh, you think you're going to stop me with a code, eh?

Well, I just happen to be the world's foremost expert on medieval codes.

She gathered the pieces of the shattered figurine in a handkerchief and tucked them away. Then she carefully copied out the code onto a sheet of paper.

Time to return to the United States, where she had her reference materials and her main computer. The tools she needed to crack this and uncover its secret.

The adventure is not over. I'm just passing through to the next step.

CHAPTER THIRTY ONE

Quantico, Virginia, three days later ...

Daniel and Remi sat in Assistant Director Ochiai's office, debriefing the professor now that she was back from her rest break in Italy. Daniel noticed that Remi looked rested and eager, flushed with excitement and positivity as if she had made some great discovery there instead of sipping wine in sidewalk cafés and visiting art galleries.

Daniel felt jealous. He could have used a vacation too, although not in Italy. Too many bad memories.

Although sometimes, hanging out with Remi, he had forgotten all that. Maybe if he had spent more time with her there, he would have forgotten it more often.

No chance to test that, though. He had come back to a mountain of paperwork involving this case.

The last bit was debriefing Remi. They had just spent an hour with Assistant Director Ochiai as she grilled Remi about every detail regarding the case. At last Daniel's boss leaned back and nodded.

"It was all in Agent Walker's report, but I wanted to hear it from the art expert too. It looks like you've done us a second favor, Professor Laurent."

"You can call me Remi."

A brief flicker of annoyance passed over the assistant director's features, so quickly Daniel almost missed it. No one got casual with Keiko Ochiai.

She didn't let it show in her tone. "We're very happy with your performance, Professor Laurent."

"Have you considered my suggestion?" Remi asked.

"We haven't come to a decision."

Daniel sensed the disappointment emanating from her.

"The way this division is shaping up," Daniel said, "I doubt this will be the last time we work together."

Remi smiled, and that made Daniel feel good.

“Probably not,” Assistant Director Ochiai conceded. “And we will keep your suggestion in mind. For the moment, however, you can go back to Georgetown and resume your teaching. Now if you’ll excuse me, I have an online meeting with the head of Scotland Yard.”

Daniel and Remi rose, thanked her, and left. They walked in silence down the hall for a minute. Finally, Daniel spoke.

“So I guess you’ll be heading up to Georgetown now,” he said. He was going to miss this annoying academic.

Remi wagged his finger at him. “Not until tomorrow. You have a promise to keep.”

“I do?”

Remi pulled out her phone. “I think I still have the search saved.”

“Search for what?”

She gave him a mischievous look over the top of her phone. “Shooting ranges.”

“Ugh. Still on that, are you? OK, fine, I’ll take you shooting, but it’s not like it is in the movies.”

“I know it’s not like in the movies,” Remi said, tapping away on her phone. “I’ve shot someone before, you know.”

“True enough. Search for ones where you can rent guns. Not all of them do that. And before you ask: no, you can’t use my sidearm. I could get fired if I let you touch it.”

Yeah, why not let her handle a gun? It was time for this professor to have a wakeup call. She had shot the killer at point blank range. She’d find shooting a man-sized target at twenty yards a bit more difficult.

Remi’s eyebrows shot up. “Here’s one, and it’s only fifteen minutes’ drive away. American Pride Guns and Ammo. Yee haw!”

“Not a bad cowboy imitation.”

“My father loved Westerns. I sat through far too many of them growing up.”

They shared a chuckle.

This is nice.

* * *

American Pride Guns and Ammo was a windowless concrete building that looked like it had once been a warehouse. A large parking lot was about a quarter full. Across the street was a liquor store and a payday loans business.

"You picked a classy place," Daniel said. "Your European refinement is really shining through."

Remi nodded. "It certainly isn't the top of the Eiffel Tower. Only snipers in the French army are allowed to practice from there."

Daniel stared at her. "Really?"

Remi laughed. "No!"

"Oh."

They went up to the front door, a blank steel rectangle with a buzzer and video camera next to it. Above the buzzer was a sign reading, "Homophobes will be shot." Remi rang the buzzer.

"Yeah?" an indifferent male voice crackled through the intercom.

"I'd like an introductory shooting class," Remi said.

"Sure, come on in girl." Daniel could recognize a Southern twang in the disembodied voice.

The door buzzed and clicked, and they pushed it open.

The interior was similar to the usual gun shops Daniel had seen—aisles of camouflage clothing and gun accessories, and plexiglass cases lining the walls filled with rifles and shotguns. A long counter along the back wall had a display of sidearms. The dozen or so customers were all men, half of them wearing some sort of camo.

Daniel saw only two things different about this place, and they made the shop very different—a male love doll in full camo (minus pants) hanging from the ceiling, and a Confederate battle flag on the wall decorated with the silhouette of crossed AR-15s and a rainbow flag background. Daniel stared at the flag for a moment. He tried to figure out what it meant and decided he couldn't.

A short man in a cowboy hat and cut-off jean vest that showed off beefy arms adorned with tattoos waved to them, smiling from under his handlebar moustache.

"Howdy! Welcome to American Pride Guns and Ammo," he said in an accent that sounded like it came from the Ozarks.

Pride. OK, I get it.

They walked up to the counter. The man behind the counter looked him up and down, tut-tutted, and turned to Remi.

"Girl, you put your man on a diet right now. Give him six months in a gym and you'll have yourself a cutie."

Daniel blushed. Remi laughed. "He's not my boyfriend."

The gun shop owner turned to Daniel. "Well, good luck for me." He pulled a business card out of his vest pocket. "This is the best gym in the city. Run by a good friend of mine. He'll work you out until you're sore."

The business card said "Adonis Gym" next to the figure of a Greek statue.

"Right now we're here to give my friend a shooting lesson. I'll take a few practice shots too. I brought my own pistol." Daniel opened his jacked to reveal the holster holding his 9mm.

"I need to see your concealed carry permit," the gun owner said.

Daniel nodded and showed him his FBI ID.

The man raised an eyebrow. "My, my, you're quite the prize. Let me show you the gun range."

The man motioned for them to follow as he headed for a steel door at the back of the store.

"You brought me to a gay shooting range?" Daniel whispered as they followed.

"Does that make you uncomfortable?" Remi asked and smiled.

"No. A bit confused, but not uncomfortable."

There was a time when he would have run out of the place. It had taken him several years to understand that regular gays and Uncle Ray were as different as he was from men who went after little girls.

That didn't mean he wanted a gun-toting hillbilly flirting with him, though.

They went down a flight of stairs closed in by blank concrete walls to another steel door. The crack of muffled gunfire could be heard from the other side. The gun shop owner picked out three pairs of noise-blocking earphones from a rack and distributed them.

When they passed through the door, they found themselves in a standard shooting range—a row of booths, each separated from the other and facing a row of targets set out at various intervals depending on the shooter's preference. A couple of the booths were occupied.

Shouting to be heard, the gun shop owner went through the basics of firearm safety and had Remi sign a waiver. As he did so, Daniel leaned against the wall and watched. He didn't see any purpose in this. It wasn't like Remi was going to carry on this case. Or ever.

Still, it was kind of fun. His ex-wife sure never wanted to come shooting with him.

Once Remi was ready, Daniel picked a booth and went to a table where they had paper targets stacked. This place offered the choice between a terrorist, a Ku Klux Klan member, or the standard silhouette. Daniel picked the Klan member.

Clipping it onto the target retriever, he pressed a button and the target retriever slid away from him on rubber wheels attached to an I-beam on the ceiling. Daniel stopped it at fifty yards and drew his Glock 17M, the FBI's standard sidearm with a seventeen-round clip of 9mm ammunition.

Daniel proceeded to empty that clip at the target.

After he shot his final round, he placed the gun on the counter in front of him and pressed the button to retrieve the target. There was a nice cluster on the torso, two head shots, one total miss, and one at the very peak of the hood. If the Klan member had a pointy enough head, that would count as a headshot too.

He felt a hand on his shoulder. He turned around to see the gun shop owner, who lifted up one of his protected earpieces and whispered,

"If you wanted to impress your girlfriend, I think you succeeded."

"She's not my girlfriend."

"Oh honey, if you looked at me like she was looking at you, I'd be whistling Dixie."

"I don't know what you mean by that, and please don't tell me."

He told Daniel anyway, but gunshots from further down the range drowned out his explanation.

Now it was Remi's turn. Under the owner's instruction, she came up to the counter, fitted a target of a terrorist on the target retriever, and put it out to ten yards.

The professor got into a proper stance and held the gun shop's .38 revolver like she knew what she was doing. Daniel nodded in appreciation. This hillbilly was a good teacher.

Slowly and methodically, she fired one round after another. Every one of them hit the target. One was even a headshot.

Daniel and the gun shop owner gaped.

"Daaang!" the hillbilly said. "You're a natural, girl."

Remi smiled and placed the revolver on the counter. "My father was a police officer in Paris. He taught me how to shoot."

She retrieved the target. "Hmmm. Looks like I'm out of practice. It's difficult for regular civilians to get guns in France. We have a shotgun and rifle at the farm. I'm better with those."

"Oh, I like this gal," the gun shop owner said, winking at Daniel. "You got to keep her."

Remi gave Daniel a satisfied smile.

"Do you think your boss will give me that permit now?" she asked.

"It's not up to her," Daniel replied.

Don't get overconfident, Remi. The last time you did that you nearly got yourself killed.

And me too.

"She'll come around," Remi said with that overconfidence that always made Daniel feel a mixture of admiration and worry. "Oh, can you come down to Georgetown sometime in the next week or so? Cyril wants to get to know you."

They had already met two days before. Cyril had come up to stay in the hotel with Remi. In separate rooms, he noticed. A bit nosey of him to notice that, but he was an FBI agent. Being nosey was part of the job description.

What wasn't part of the job description was the smug satisfaction that gave him. He hadn't delved into that feeling too much. He had a job to do.

They had a job to do.

And it gave him a great deal of satisfaction to know they would keep on doing it.

Because the file that Assistant Director Ochiai had handed him earlier that day was about a case that he stood no chance of doing alone.

He wasn't even sure Remi and him together could tackle it.

"Better fire off another few clips," Daniel said. "You might need the practice."

CHAPTER THIRTY TWO

Georgetown University, the next day

Remi didn't know whether to laugh or cry.

Sitting in her office with the door closed for privacy, she had just gotten an email from Francesco Costa, the self-styled "most famous astrologer in Sicily."

"Dear Dr. Laurent,

I have just cast a horoscope based on the photographs of the four paintings you provided. This took quite some time, as I had to base my findings not on the modern science of astrology, but on the superstitions of the century in which they were painted.

"They do, as you suggested, provide a date for the Apocalypse. I do not know if you are a religious woman and whether such a date would hold any significance to you, but I am a devout Catholic. Despite the criticisms of the Church, I do not see a contradiction between my science and the teachings of the church. For did not God make the stars and planets? Why wouldn't He put secrets in their arrangement and movements?

"So I, and perhaps you, can take comfort in the fact that the paintings do not predict the End Times to be upon us until the year 2500. One wonders if we will bring this date forward not through God's plan, but our own actions. I'd like to think not, but then I read the newspaper.

"Thank you for the fascinating opportunity to study these paintings and the secret they have hidden for all this time. Also, I found that your name was familiar, and I looked you up. Your research into the cryptex is intriguing. Do you know if your book and papers on the subject will ever be translated into Italian? I would love to read them.

"Perhaps, someday, someone using your research as inspiration, will eventually find the cryptex. Who knows what secrets it might hold?

"Yours sincerely, Francesco Costa"

Who indeed! Remi couldn't decide what was funnier, the fact that such a madman was so desperate to find the date of the Apocalypse, only for the paintings to put it off for another five centuries, or that "the most famous astrologer in Sicily" thinks that "someday" someone would find the cryptex using her research.

Well, she had found the cryptex, and unlocked it, and now she was faced with the puzzle it had led her to. A series of letters and numbers arranged seemingly at random. This was going to be a tough nut to crack.

In fact, she had been trying to crack it ever since that day in Italy, barely a week but seemingly a lifetime ago. She was growing more and more frustrated at her lack of progress, despite her skill in dealing with medieval codes.

Patience, Remi. Patience. You'll get there in the end.

A quiet knock came at her office door. She quickly closed her email and brought up a journal article she had been reading.

Then she composed herself, got up, and opened the door. It was her boyfriend, Cyril.

Despite the late hour, he glanced both ways down the hall to make sure no one was looking before giving her a kiss. American universities frowned on faculty members dating. Some things about this country she would never understand.

"Come on in. I'm just reading," she said.

She felt a bit guilty about not telling Cyril about her discoveries. It seemed odd that the most important man in her life would be cut off from her research. Sad to say, he had never taken it seriously, and their relationship had been a bit rocky these past few weeks.

Cyril sensed it too, because he had been quiet and cautious around her since that blowup in the restaurant. They had kissed, embraced, but hadn't made love.

"So the case is all finished?" he asked.

Remi sat down at her desk again. "Yes. The killer was an upper-class man from New York who became obsessed with astrology and predictions of the Apocalypse. His house was filled with macabre art."

"Like all those German Renaissance woodcuts of witch burnings?"

"Dozens of them. He would have had the complete set of Goya's *caprichos* if he could have afforded them."

"Good thing he wasn't a multimillionaire," Cyril said with a faint smile. He sat tentatively at the edge of her desk. It was odd to see such a strong man so indecisive. "So … will there be another case?"

I hope so. "I don't know."

"But probably."

"Yes, probably."

"I'm … sorry I've been so unsupportive of this new, um, venture of yours. It's just that you've gotten so focused on it."

"I'm not giving up my career as a historian," Remi said, heading off the usual criticism.

But today he didn't say his usual thing. Looking briefly into her eyes and then back at the floor, he said, "It's just that these cases keep taking you away from Georgetown. I'm afraid they'll take you away for good."

Remi felt her heart go out to him. This man had gone through a terrible divorce, with a woman who immediately ran off with a younger man who she had most likely been seeing before the marriage ended. Other than his daughter, Cyril had no one close in his life.

No one but her.

Of course, he was frightened of losing her. That's why he had pressured her so much to get married as soon as possible.

She still didn't know what she thought of that.

Remi reached out and took his hand. He looked up from the floor.

"This is a good thing. The FBI said that they can extend my visa after my time here is up. I can continue my work as an independent researcher while being on retainer for the FBI. Don't you see? I can stay!"

Cyril's eyes lit up with a tentative hope, then clouded into uncertainty.

"But they could end that at any time."

What you mean to say is if we get married, then I can stay for good.

Remi stood and put her arms on his shoulders.

"I'm not going anywhere, Cyril." She kissed him softly on the lips.

He smiled, a heartfelt smile this time.

"I'm glad. It's just that I want to be let in more. When you get on these cases it's like you disappear, not just physically but in all ways. I want to help. Well, not chase serial killers." He laughed, and so did she. "But I want to be there for you. You can't do it all alone."

His phone buzzed.

"Damn." He checked his messages. "It's one of my grad students. I completely forgot I was to meet him. I'm late. You have time later tonight?"

"I always have time for you, Cyril. How about I make a reservation at Perla di Napoli? My treat. And we'll do it right this time."

"All right." He kissed her again. His phone buzzed a second time.

Remi shrugged. "Grad students. So impatient."

"Got to go. Eight o'clock?"

"I'll be there."

Cyril left, and Remi closed her door again, feeling much better. He was a good man, and most of his flaws came from the wounds that horrible woman had given him. She promised herself to be more patient with their relationship from now on.

Remi sat back down at her desk and started staring at the scan of the code she had made. What a mess. A seemingly random series of letter and numbers. It would take ages to crack.

And she worried that the Church might get to the solution first. They had the original cryptex and its secret map, after all.

Of course, they didn't have what she had, she thought with smug satisfaction, but with their centuries of secret archives and knowledge, they might not need it. They might be able to skip right over to the final revelation.

She needed to break this code sooner rather than later.

But how? Codes like this often took months or even years to solve.

You can't do it all alone. That's what Cyril had said.

She hadn't done it all alone in this last case. Daniel had helped her. And so had the police. Even that silly little Sicilian had lent a hand.

So who could help her with this?

As soon as she asked the question, the answer became obvious.

There was a scholar at the University of Toronto who was just as brilliant at cracking codes as she was. While he worked in a later period, studying the codes of early modern times such as those used by the armies of the Napoleonic Wars, a code was a code. With his genius and her knowledge of the period, they'd make a great team.

And he'd be more than willing to help.

That, unfortunately, posed a problem. He'd be all too willing.

They'd had a fling a few years ago, before Cyril. He had been anxious to continue but she had put him off. The physical separation was too great. She didn't want a long-distance relationship.

Would he understand that and be willing to put his feelings aside? She hoped so. This was a tempting puzzle, and he loved puzzles as much as she did.

Cyril was right. She couldn't go it alone, not if she wanted to solve this.

Remi paused. But to bring her ex-lover aboard, she'd need to tell him she had found the cryptex. She'd need to tell him about stealing from a church in Italy.

Did she? Well, she could leave out some of the more awkward details, but a large part of cryptography was knowing the context. The Allies couldn't have broken the Enigma machine if they hadn't known the Germans were using it to transmit military orders and troop movements.

So an ex-lover would have to know what her current lover did not. That could be dangerous.

But this whole hunt had been dangerous, and this was the only way forward.

Putting her fears aside, she looked up the professor's number and made the call.

NOW AVAILABLE FOR PRE-ORDER!

THE MALICE CODE
(A Remi Laurent FBI Suspense Thriller—Book 3)

THE MALICE CODE (A Remi Laurent FBI Suspense Thriller) is book #3 in a new series by mystery and suspense author Ava Strong, which begins with THE DEATH CODE (Book #1).

FBI Special Agent Daniel Walker, 40, known for his ability to hunt killers, his street-smarts, and his disobedience, is singled out from the Behavioral Analysis Unit and assigned to the FBI's new Antiquities unit. The unit, formed to hunt down priceless relics in the global world of antiquities, has no idea how to enter the mind of a murderer.

Remi Laurent, 34, brilliant history professor at Georgetown, is the world's leading expert in obscure historic artifacts. Shocked when the FBI asks for her help to find a killer, she finds herself reluctantly partnered with this rude American FBI agent. Special Agent Walker and Remi Laurent are an unlikely duo, with his ability to enter killers' minds and her unparalleled scholarship, the only thing they have in common, their determination to decode the clues and stop a killer.

When an American is found murdered in Italy, the victim of a potential serial killer obsessed with ancient church relics, the FBI's Antiquities unit is summoned to help. Special Agent Walker knows he needs Remi's scholarship to decode the undecipherable puzzle that leads them in a wild race across Italy, from the secrets of the Vatican to forgotten churches in Tuscany.

Together, they must follow the clues, peel back the layers of history, and solve the riddle before the killer strikes again.

But will they be too late?

An unputdownable crime thriller featuring an unlikely partnership between a jaded FBI agent and a brilliant historian, the REMI LAURENT series is a riveting mystery, grounded in history, and packed with suspense and revelations that will leave you continuously in shock, and flipping pages late into the night.

Future books in the series will be available soon.

Ava Strong

Debut author Ava Strong is author of the REMI LAURENT mystery series, comprising three books (and counting); of the ILSE BECK mystery series, comprising four books (and counting); and of the STELLA FALL psychological suspense thriller series, comprising three books (and counting).

An avid reader and lifelong fan of the mystery and thriller genres, Ava loves to hear from you, so please feel free to visit http://www.avastrongauthor.com to learn more and stay in touch.

BOOKS BY AVA STRONG

REMI LAURENT FBI SUSPENSE THRILLER
THE DEATH CODE (Book #1)
THE MURDER CODE (Book #2)
THE MALICE CODE (Book #3)

ILSE BECK FBI SUSPENSE THRILLER
NOT LIKE US (Book #1)
NOT LIKE HE SEEMED (Book #2)
NOT LIKE YESTERDAY (Book #3)
NOT LIKE THIS (Book #4)

STELLA FALL PSYCHOLOGICAL SUSPENSE THRILLER
HIS OTHER WIFE (Book #1)
HIS OTHER LIE (Book #2)
HIS OTHER SECRET (Book #3)

www.ingramcontent.com/pod-product-compliance
Lightning Source LLC
Chambersburg PA
CBHW030617310726
48979CB00003B/760

9781094392950